The Broken Bridge

Philip Pullman is the acclaimed author of novels, short stories and plays for readers of all ages. He has received many awards for his books for young people. *Northern Lights*, the first book in the His Dark Materials trilogy, won the 1996 Carnegie Medal, the Guardian Children's Fiction Award and the British Book Award. *The Firework-Maker's Daughter* won the 1996 Smarties Gold Award. *Clockwork* was shortlisted for the Whitbread Children's Book of the Year, 1997, and for the Carnegie Medal.

His other books include *The Subtle Knife* and *The Amber Spyglass* – the second and third books in the His Dark Materials trilogy. *The Amber Spyglass* was the first children's book to win the Whitbread Book of the Year in 2001. Philip Pullman is also the winner of the Astrid Lindgren Memorial Award 2005.

Praise for *The Broken Bridge*:

'The emotional truths that Pullman reveals are so heartfelt and raw that they hardly read like fiction. A spellbinding yarn from an accomplished author' *Publishers' Weekly*

'A credit to the storytelling skill of Philip Pullman . . . As the plot tumbles forward, the writing remains fresh, the settings original and the central characters compelling' *New York Times*

'A clever and sympath⸺ ⸺ ⸺ovel, full of solid characters ⸺ *Guardian*

'Almost impossible to p⸺

Also by Philip Pullman

How to Be Cool
The Butterfly Tattoo

The Sally Lockhart Quartet
The Ruby in the Smoke
The Shadow in the North
The Tiger in the Well
The Tin Princess

His Dark Materials
1. Northern Lights
2. The Subtle Knife
3. The Amber Spyglass
Lyra's Oxford

Books for younger readers
Spring-Heeled Jack
Count Karlstein
The Wonderful Story of Aladdin and the
Enchanted Lamp
The Firework-Maker's Daughter
Clockwork, or All Wound Up
Thunderbolt's Waxwork
The Gas-Fitters' Ball
I Was a Rat!
Puss in Boots
Mossycoat
The Scarecrow and His Servant

PHILIP PULLMAN

The Broken Bridge

YOUNG PICADOR

First published 1990 by Macmillan Children's Books

This revised edition published 2004 by Young Picador
an imprint of Pan Macmillan Limited
20 New Wharf Road, London N1 9RR
Basingstoke and Oxford
www.panmacmillan.com

Associated companies throughout the world

ISBN-13: 978-0-330-39797-1
ISBN-10: 0-330-39797-4

Copyright © Philip Pullman 1990

The right of Philip Pullman to be identified as the
author of this work has been asserted by him in
accordance with the Copyright, Designs and Patents Act 1988.

15 17 19 20 18 16

A CIP catalogue record for this book is available from
the British Library.

Phototypeset by Intype Libra Ltd
Printed and bound in Great Britain by Mackays of Chatham plc, Kent

One day in the school playground they'd said, *Eeny, meeny, miny, Mo, Catch a nigger by his toe,* and they'd all looked at Ginny and laughed. They called her Eeny Meeny after that.

In the bath she told Dad to wash her harder.

'Why?' he said. 'You're as clean as a whistle.'

'I'm dirty,' she said.

'You're not dirty, silly.'

'But I'm not the same as them. I want to be the same colour. They call me Eeny Meeny.'

'You're the right colour for you, and they're the right colour for them,' said Dad.

She wanted to say, Well, why is it right for me to be different from everyone else? *Even Dad was white like them. But he kissed her and wrapped her in the towel and dried her hard, and she couldn't talk till she'd forgotten what she was going to say. They stopped calling her Eeny Meeny, though.*

1

Chapter One
The visitor

One hot day towards the end of the summer term in which Ginny had her sixteenth birthday, she got home from school to find Dad already there, talking to a stranger. Normally he didn't get home till six or so, by which time she'd have done her homework and peeled the potatoes or made a salad or prepared whatever else they'd decided to have for supper. He hadn't told her that he'd be home today; she heard voices as she came through the kitchen, and her heart beat nervously for a moment.

She found them in the living room. Dad was looking preoccupied, and there was a woman in a suit, who smiled and held out her hand to be shaken, so Ginny automatically shook it.

'This is Wendy Stevens,' said Dad.

Wendy Stevens was big, or fat actually, Ginny thought, with lots of blond hair elaborately waved like a country and western singer's. Her suit was dark blue, and she wore blusher and eye shadow, and her forehead was gleaming with the heat. When she spoke she smiled at the same time. She was very friendly, asking Ginny about school and hobbies and sports and fashions and pop music in a way that, after five minutes, began to make Ginny feel puzzled and rebellious. Dad had gone out to the kitchen; Ginny could tell he was relieved to get away.

Finally she said, 'Who are you anyway? Are you a friend of Dad's?'

'No, I work for the Social Services Department,' she said. 'Not locally. In Liverpool.'

'Are you a social worker?' Ginny was suspicious at once.

'Sort of. Why? Don't you like social workers?'

'I don't know any,' she said. 'Why are you asking me all these questions?'

'Just getting to know you,' said Wendy Stevens, smiling.

'Well, you won't find out much by . . . I mean, sports and fashion and pop music . . . It's not *me*, really.'

'Your dad's told me about your hobby.'

'Hobby?'

'Drawing. Painting.'

'That's not a hobby,' said Ginny severely. 'I don't want to be rude, but . . . what are you doing here anyway?'

'Does it worry you?'

'Yeah. Are you checking up or something?'

'What would I be checking up on?'

'Dunno. Anything.'

'What sort of things?'

This was a stupid game, Ginny thought. Then something came into her mind and made her shiver: there'd been a case in the news recently where the social services had been criticized for failing to remove a child from the care of her father, who'd been abusing her. And there'd been another case where they had split a family up, and it turned out that the father hadn't done anything at all . . . But was that why Wendy Stevens was here? Did they think she was being abused? Did they think that was more likely to happen where there wasn't a mother? Would they take her away from Dad?

She stood up and moved to the window that overlooked the tiny front garden and the fields leading down to the sea. You could never tell. She didn't know how much power social workers had; they seemed to be able to take children into custody whether or not the parents objected. But it was ridiculous. They couldn't believe that Dad was doing anything like that to her. It was impossible.

'You look as if you've seen a ghost,' said Wendy Stevens. 'Am I that bad?'

The door opened, and Dad came in with a tray

of mugs of tea and some biscuits. There *was* something the matter; Ginny could tell. She wanted to get out and go down to the beach, but she thought she'd better stay and show there was nothing wrong between her and Dad. If Wendy Stevens could see that everything was normal, she might go away and leave them alone.

So Ginny sat down again, passed the biscuits, talked about school; and presently Wendy Stevens looked at her watch and began to put away the papers Ginny noticed for the first time. She had a cherry-red plastic briefcase with green canvas webbing at the corners; a tattered sticker on it said SUPPORT THE DOCKERS.

'Nice to meet you, Ginny,' she said as she stood up. 'Hope we see each other again.'

She shook hands. Ginny smiled and nodded, and cleared the mugs and plates away as Dad went out with the woman to the Renault 5 parked in the lane.

'What did she want?' Ginny said when Dad came back. 'She was asking all kinds of questions. All stupid ones, about pop music and stuff. Patronizing.'

'How d'you know she wasn't my new girlfriend?' Dad said.

''Cause you've got better taste.'

He smiled, but there was still something wrong.

He went to the sink and started washing the mugs.

'But what *was* it?' Ginny said again.

'Oh, it was some nonsense . . . D'you remember when we lived in Liverpool?'

'Was that the basement where you slept next to the fridge?'

'Next to the fridge? Oh, no, that was Hammersmith. When we lived in Liverpool, the Social Services helped out when I had to work late. There was a sort of nursery place. And Wendy Whatsername worked there, so she remembered you.'

'But did she come all this way just to see us again?'

'No. We're not that famous. She was on her way back from a conference in Aberystwyth and just dropped in to say hello. Nothing important.'

Oh, yeah, Ginny thought. But she didn't say it. Instead she wandered back to the living room, took out her schoolbooks, and began the last French homework before her exam.

Apart from art, French was her best subject. She considered it to be her native language, her mother tongue, her mother's tongue. She'd never learned it from her mother, who had died a week or so after Ginny was born, but Ginny was proud of it all the same; just as she was proud of her mother and the colour she'd inherited and the exoticness in her blood. Her father was English, white, but her mother had come from Haiti, where they spoke French and Creole, so Ginny applied herself to French with love and ardour: it belonged to her in the way that Welsh belonged to the other kids at school. Ginny had to learn Welsh too, and she did it conscientiously, but it felt cramped and alien. In French she was at home.

So normally she'd have worked at this exercise with pleasure, maybe imagining the day when she, speaking French perfectly, would be studying art in Paris or seeking out long-lost cousins in Haiti; but not today. Something was wrong. Dad wasn't telling the truth.

She gazed at the line of sand dunes a mile or so away, wondering if someone had told the Social Services that Dad was abusing her. She thought it must be that. One of the neighbours? But on one side lived Mr and Mrs Price, a retired stationmaster and his disabled wife, and on the other side were the Laxtons and their bed-and-breakfast . . . Of course not. They were good people. Ridiculous. She went back to the French, listening to the sounds of Dad in the kitchen, the radio, the knife on the chopping board, the kettle boiling.

*

Ginny's dad owned his own business, setting up computer systems for offices and factories and advising people how to run the ones they had. He'd never remarried after Ginny's mother died. Now, at the age of thirty-seven, he looked as if he came from an earlier time; without being ridiculously handsome, he had the sort of looks you could see in film stars of the thirties and forties. He had black hair and bright blue eyes, and if he put a spotted handkerchief around his head, a gold ring in one ear, and a dagger between his teeth, he could have played alongside Gene Kelly in *The Pirate*, which Ginny had watched on TV over Christmas.

He and Ginny were close, almost like brother and sister, like equals. Despite her dark skin, her African features, you could see they were related: there was something of his mocking energy in her gaze. He was proud of her, proud of her talent, proud of her diligence; and she was proud of him, of his energy, his attractiveness. He had many girlfriends. Ginny used to think of them as the breakfast ladies, because sometimes she'd come down to breakfast and there would be a strange young woman she'd never seen before. She thought they just came for breakfast until she realized that they stayed all night, but she didn't realize why they stayed all night until much later, when there was only one of them. She was called Holly, and she stayed six months, and Ginny, feeling that they ought to be respectable, wanted to know if she and Dad were going to get married. But shortly afterwards Holly left.

Ginny didn't feel jealous, because Dad always included her in things. When he took one of the breakfast ladies out for a meal, Ginny came, too, and learned to be sophisticated. When it was another's birthday, Ginny chose a present for her. And she and Dad talked about them: how Annie loved to gorge herself on fried bread and bacon, how Teresa hardly ate anything, how Mair used to sing hymns in the shower.

They were all white, of course. Not that Ginny expected Dad to have a black lover just because Maman had been black – in this part of Wales there were hardly any black faces to be seen – but when things were difficult, that was part of the difficulty. It was always there, being a black person in a white world, from the time she'd first become aware of it: Eeny Meeny – she grew hot at the thought. But it hadn't been urgent. Well, it wasn't urgent now, but she was sixteen, and though she thought she was pretty and Dad told her she was pretty and though her friends reassured her too, nevertheless, boys . . . well, they were cowards anyway. Which one of them would want to mark himself out from the rest by going out with a black girl? She knew that was how they'd feel. She guessed that was why no one had asked her. And if they did ask, they'd resent her for making them feel like that, so there'd always be other feelings mixed up with the relationship. She'd put the thought aside, into the darkness, but it hadn't gone away; she could sense it there, awake, and one day she'd have to deal with it.

'Supper's ready,' Dad called.

'I'm not hungry,' she said quietly, but she went anyway.

'Dad, what *was* she here for?' she said over the grilled lamb chops and salad.

'Nothing. Just passing.'

'But this isn't the way to Liverpool from Aberystwyth.'

'She might be going somewhere else for the weekend. Who knows? Who cares?'

'I thought she was stupid.'

'I expect she noticed,' he said.

'What d'you mean?'

'Well, you're not very tactful, are you?'

'Me?'

'You were looking at her as if she was poison.'

'I wasn't . . .'

'Well, it probably doesn't matter. I don't suppose she'll come again.'

'She had a load of papers all spread out. Was it something about me?'

'No, of course not. D'you want to finish the salad?'

After they'd eaten and she'd washed the dishes, she went out and wandered down the lane towards the beach. The house stood between its two neighbours in this little side lane off the road that led down to the sea from the main route along the coast. Inland, on the far side of the main road, a range of great grass-covered hills, not quite mountains but as high as hills could get, rolled endlessly away out of sight; but on this side, the seaward side, there was a space of magic and beauty, Ginny's realm, her kingdom, her queendom.

It was a mile wide: all the land between the main road and the sea. There was a grassy field below the road, then the lane with her house, then more fields, then a railway line, then another field and the sand dunes and the beach. To the right there was a parking area and a little shop, and a tiny caravan site that you couldn't see from the house; and to the left there was an estuary, where a little river, which only a few miles back in the hills was tumbling swiftly among rocks, spread itself out wide and slow through a tidal lagoon. Beyond that there were more dunes and, at the very edge of the horizon, an airfield from which tiny silver planes occasionally took off, to skim over the sea and vanish. Everything from the airfield to the caravan site, from the main road to the edge of the sea, was Ginny's.

She owned it, first, because she knew it: during the years they'd lived here, she'd wandered all over this gently sloping margin, this halfway place between the hills and the sea. She owned it because she'd drawn it, from the insects on the dry-stone walls to the decaying church half-buried in the dunes to the little bridge that carried the railway line over the estuary. And she owned it, finally, because she loved it. Everyone who entered this kingdom became a subject of hers without knowing it, owing her allegiance, paying her invisible respect. Nothing bad was permitted to happen in Ginny's kingdom; she was in charge; she saw to it.

So now as she wandered down the lane she looked over everything, inspecting the landscape as if it were a guard of honour. The ancient round stones in the walls, grey and lichen-covered, the grass in the fields, brown and dry from the weeks of hot weather, the coppery sun, still with an hour or two's light to shed before sinking into the sea – it was all in place, all as it should be.

There were still quite a few people on the beach, though some of them were beginning to pack away their sandy picnic boxes and their wet towels and their gritty, oily suntan bottles and make stiffly for the parking area. Ginny wandered along the soft sand to the right, above the rock pools where children were still crouching, intently fishing for little transparent shrimps, for crabs and starfish. The late golden light tinted everything evenly, benevolently, and the sea folded neat little waves quietly over on to the flat sand.

'Ginny!'

It was a stage whisper rather than a shout, and she couldn't place the voice, but then a lazy hand went up on the slope of the dunes to her right.

'Andy! What're you doing back?'

She threw herself to her knees beside him, too pleased and happy to do more than grin. Andy was two years older than she was, which was a lot, of course, and he'd left school the previous term and gone away somewhere. In the whole school, his had been the only other black face. He was mysterious, glamorous with a kind of evasive magic, half spirit, half conman. He was much darker than Ginny, both his parents having been African; but he'd been adopted by a white couple in the town eight miles to the south, and that gave them something else in common: looking black, they'd each grown up feeling white.

Ginny had only got to know Andy properly in the past year or so, and then he'd vanished. And now he was back, and she was so happy she didn't know what to say.

'How you doing, then?' he said, lying back with his hands under his head. 'You got a boyfriend yet?'

'Shut up,' she said. 'I don't want a boyfriend. Where you been?'

'In Bristol,' he said. 'Catering college. I know it all now. Mayonnaise, wine, *carbonnade de boeuf,* opening sardine tins – I can do anything.'

'Has the term finished or something?'

'No. *I* finished. I might go back sometime, learn a bit more, but I got a job in the Castle.'

'The Castle?' There was a battered little ruin in the town a mile or two up the coast, but Ginny had no idea that anyone worked there.

'The Castle Hotel. In the kitchen. It's a right laugh. Carlos, the chef there, he's got all kinds of scams, all kinds of rackets going on . . . I'm getting a caravan, how about that?'

'A caravan? Aren't you living at home?'

'Well, that got a bit dodgy. They don't know I'm back. No, me and Dafydd Lewis from the garage, we're going to share this caravan. We're putting it in old man Alston's field just back there.'

Ginny had never seen Andy's adoptive parents,

but she'd heard that they were elderly and strict. If Andy was going to be living just behind the dunes, everything was going to be wonderful, brilliant. She knew the field he meant: it belonged to the richest man in the county, who owned factories and garden centres and printing works. Dad had done some work for him. He was having a house built in the field, but not very quickly. Every few weeks some men would drive down in a truck and unload timber or bricks or drainpipes and go away again, and by the time the workmen arrived to do something with them, half the materials would be missing. No one seemed to mind.

'Does he know?' Ginny said.

'What, old man Alston? He won't know. Oh, we'll have some good times this summer, Gin. You wait and see . . . Aye, aye, watch out!'

He rolled over on to his stomach, facing away from the beach, and laid his head on his hands.

'What?' Ginny looked around to see who he was hiding from.

'Bloke down there with a leather jacket,' Andy muttered. 'Big belly on him.'

The man was plodding through the sand below them. He was heavy-looking, and the leather jacket he wore added to his bulk, but the most remarkable thing was his head. It seemed almost inhumanly large, the features coarse and blunt like a giant's, and everything the same sandy colour: lips, eyebrows, thin greasy hair.

'What's he doing?' Andy said.

'He's stopped – he's looking the other way – now he's going up to the car park. There, he's gone. Who is he?'

'Joe Chicago,' said Andy, rolling over again. 'Gangster, he is. From Aberystwyth.'

Ginny found herself giggling at the idea of a gangster called Joe Chicago coming from Aberystwyth. Andy shook his head.

'You can laugh,' he said solemnly.

'Where's his gang, then?' Ginny said.

'Oh, he hasn't got a gang.'

'But that's what gangster means – having a gang!'

'Yeah, maybe. But he's a soloist.'

'Why's he after you?'

'Oh . . .' He shrugged, and for the first time in Ginny's experience, Andy looked embarrassed. The expression sat so strangely on his face that for a moment she mistook it for fear. But no, she thought, not Andy, he wouldn't be afraid of anything, surely?

The moment passed like a small cloud drifting over the sun, and then Andy was sitting up again as if nothing had happened.

'Hey,' he said, flicking her knee, 'you want a job?'

'After the end of term, yeah, I wouldn't mind. What sort of job?'

'In the Yacht Club. Angie Lime needs someone in the kitchen and laying the tables and that. I said I might lend a hand meself, but you know, I'm a busy man, I might get overstressed. Could be fatal.'

Anyone less likely than Andy to die of stress hadn't been born, she thought. 'OK,' she said. 'I wouldn't want you to run the risk of that. Is it every day?'

'Evenings. Six till eight. I'll tell her, shall I? I'm going over there later. Doing the rounds, you know, visiting my flock, giving them their little touch of Andy for the day.'

'Yeah. Tell her. I'll go and see her myself. That's great!'

The Yacht Club in the estuary wasn't a club at all, it was the Harbour Restaurant, but the Welsh were inventive with names. Angie Lime was only called that because her husband's name was Harry. Consequently, he wasn't Harry Williams, his real name, but Harry Lime, as in *The Third Man*, and she was Angie Lime. They'd had the Yacht Club for a year or so. Ginny and Dad had been there for a meal; it was small and friendly and bistro-like, and Angie was a good cook. It would be fun working

there. It would be fun having Andy around. Everything was good suddenly, everything was fun,
everything was as it should be in her mile-wide
kingdom by the sea, as the last visitors trudged up
through the soft sand towards their cars and the
waves kept falling neatly and the sun sank towards
the edge of the world in a welter of blood-red sky.

'Dad? You know Andy?'

'Andy Evans? I saw him today. He was talking to
Dafydd in the garage. Why?'

'Well, he said they needed someone to help in
the Yacht Club, in the kitchen, right, and I said I'd
do it. In the evenings.'

'What, the whole evening? Aren't I going to see
you at all?'

It was late. Dad was lying in the hammock in the
hot night, with something by Mozart playing very
quietly through the open window and the underside
of the leaves lit up above him by the floodlight at
the base of the tree. He often lay in the hammock.
Sometimes he slept out all night. Sometimes she
joined him, bringing her mattress and duvet out
under the stars. It was going to be hot enough for
that tonight, but there was a distance between them
now, after Wendy Stevens' visit.

Ginny reclined the deck chair to its limit and sat

down, not far away, gazing up at the canopy of leaves, the lightest viridian against the velvet black.

'Only from six till eight o'clock,' she said.

'Well, that sounds all right. D'you want to?'

'Yeah. That's why I said I would.'

'So you did. How much are they going to pay you?'

'I don't know. I haven't actually spoken to them yet.'

'Counting your chickens again,' he said.

'Well, maybe.'

They sat companionably, without talking, for a few more minutes. The Mozart tape came to an end and clicked off.

'You ought to have your Walkman on,' she said. 'Then you wouldn't have to keep getting up to turn the tape over.'

'I don't have to. I ask you nicely, and you do it for me.'

'You reckon?' she said, getting up.

'No worries.'

'D'you want the other side?'

'No. Chopin Nocturnes. The Rubinstein one.'

She went in, found the tape, set it going.

'I still think it'd be easier with the Walkman,' she said, outside again.

'I don't want to shut the rest of the world out. I

want to hear the music coming quietly from a distance, with all the night around it. As if you're hearing it through the open windows of a great house across a lake . . .'

'Yah! Pretentious twit!' she said, but the image secretly delighted her, and she pictured it to herself, composing the scene in her mind like a painting. She could see it taking shape; her imagination worked effortlessly, taking what it needed from every memory she had of classical buildings, and lawns, and light reflected off dark water. Unlike memories of people, memories of things came easily to her; she had only to think of an object or a place to find it before her, correctly textured, three-dimensional, casting shadows. There were a lot of things about herself she didn't know, and one was how rare this gift was, though she was beginning to sense it.

She lay back in the warm night, in the magic circle of light under the old tree with Chopin coming faintly across the imaginary lake, with her beloved father close by, and felt unbearably rich. She loved him so much. The world was so full, so strange, and she and Dad understood each other so well; this was how it should be for ever.

Chapter Two
Rhiannon's sister

On the first afternoon of the summer holiday, Ginny's best friend, Rhiannon, came to see her and told her something strange.

Rhiannon lived in the town a couple of miles up the coast, where her parents ran a café called the Dragon. Ginny liked them; Mr Calvert was a bouncy, eccentric man given to sudden enthusiasms, such as sailing or playing the guitar, which he'd take up and pursue passionately for a few months and then suddenly drop, whereas Mrs Calvert was patient and sensible. Ginny enjoyed being at the Calverts' because among other things they were a family, they were complete. And she liked Rhiannon, who was vain and languid and funny and kind.

That Monday afternoon, while Dad was out at work, Ginny and Rhiannon went down to the beach and tried to swim in the chilly water, and then lay in the scorching sun before drifting back to the house and sitting in the garden.

Rhiannon lay in the hammock, her long dark hair

drifting silkily over the edge. Ginny had often tried to draw her, but she'd never succeeded in getting her sinuous lethargic grace on to the paper. You needed to be someone like Burne-Jones for that, she thought, having just read a book about the Pre-Raphaelites; for herself, she preferred Picasso or Van Gogh. Only they'd have been able to draw her too. Keep trying.

They lay under the trees talking idly, and then Rhiannon said, 'Oh! I know what I was going to tell you. My sister rang up yesterday.'

'Your sister? I never knew you had a sister!'

Ginny was amazed. She'd always thought of Rhiannon as an only child like herself.

'Yeah, well, they don't talk about her much. She's a lot older than me – she's twenty-six or something. She left home; I mean, they threw her out, I think. There was some kind of quarrel when I was young. A terrible row. I don't know what it was about, but they've never spoken about her since . . .'

'Wow, that's incredible,' said Ginny, trying to imagine a quarrel as bitter as that. 'What's her name? Why did she ring up?'

'She's called Helen. She rang up to ask about you, actually.'

Ginny sat up to see if Rhiannon was joking. She was simply lying there languidly, trailing a hand through the dry grass beneath the hammock, gazing up with half-closed eyes through the sunny leaves above her. She turned to look at Ginny.

'It's true,' she said. 'Mam answered the phone, OK, and she didn't recognize Helen's voice. Well, she wouldn't, probably. She came in the living room and said it was for me, so I went out and shut the door 'cause I thought it might be Peter; he said he'd ring. And this strange woman's voice said, "Listen, don't sound surprised, I don't want Mam and Dad to know, this is Helen, your sister." Well, *Duw annwyl*, I didn't know what to say, you know – it was like a voice from the grave or something. I said, "Where are you?" And she said, "At home in Porthafon." '

Porthafon was a town about twenty miles up the coast. Ginny was sitting upright now, watching Rhiannon bright-eyed.

'And you never knew she was living there?'

'I told you, we never speak about her. I didn't really know she was living at all. She gave me her address, Twelve Jubilee Terrace. She said she was married. Her husband's called Benny something – Meredith, I think. He sells double glazing. And she works in an architect's office. They've got no children. She told me all that kind of thing; she sounded really nice, really friendly. I couldn't believe who I was listening to, you know. She kept saying, "You're sure they're not listening? They can't hear me?" as if she was scared.'

'Scared? I can't imagine anyone being scared of your mam and dad. But what did she say about me?'

'Oh, yes, right, I was coming to that. Well, she asked what class I was in at school, and I told her, and she said did I know a girl called Ginny Howard? I said yeah, and she said . . .' Rhiannon paused a moment and seemed to be adjusting her position, or avoiding Ginny's eye, before going on: 'She said were you adopted?'

'*What?*'

'That's what she said. So I said no, course not. I told her what, you know, what you've told me, about your mam and all that . . .'

'But why did she want to know?' Ginny was bemused. 'How did she know about me anyway?'

'Well, I asked her that, course I did. She just said she'd met your dad, see. And she was curious about you, I suppose. She probably fancies him. Hey, if she leaves her husband and marries your dad, you'll have to call me auntie.'

Ginny smiled, but she wasn't sure how she felt about this stranger asking questions about her. She supposed it might be flattering, if you felt confident about yourself. You might assume that someone was asking about you because you were attractive or interesting; she was sure Rhiannon would feel like that. But Ginny didn't; she felt threatened.

Then she felt that Rhiannon had something else to say. She looked up and saw the other girl blushing.

'And then she said . . .' Rhiannon began. 'This is crazy; you won't believe this. She said was it true that your dad had been in prison?'

Now Ginny felt really stupid. She knew she was gaping, she even felt her mouth open and thought: *So your jaw really does drop*, but she could find nothing whatever to say.

'I told her no, course not, what a stupid idea,' Rhiannon went on, 'and she said no, it didn't seem very likely. Something like that. So I asked her where she heard that from, and she said, "Oh, someone in town." Mam came out then, and I had to say goodbye.'

'Prison?' said Ginny. 'That's ridiculous. Why? What's he supposed to have done?'

'I don't know! 'Cause *she* didn't know. She only heard this rumour, and she wanted to find out more, I suppose. It must be a mistake. Oh! I knew there was something else. Dad says d'you want a job? Just in the morning, doing coffees, laying tables for lunch.'

'Everyone's offering me jobs,' said Ginny.

'Who else is, then?'

'The Yacht Club. You know Andy's back? Andy Evans? He told me about it. I'm going to work there in the evenings.'

'Well, don't tell Dad. He thinks Harry Lime's trying to pinch all our customers – you know how he gets obsessed. Mam thinks he's crazy, because they're different sorts of customers anyway, and everyone knows Angie Lime's a good cook. You going to come and work in the Dragon, then? Be a laugh anyway.'

'Yeah. Tell him I will. And thanks. When do I start?'

'Tomorrow, if you want.'

'Great . . . Rhiannon, is your sister going to ring up again?'

'I don't know. She might. I want to meet her, but I'm nervous, you know?'

'So do I want to meet her,' said Ginny.

'Oh, hey, listen, I'm not supposed to've told you, OK? She said, "Don't tell her." So . . .'

'But I want to find out what it's about! And I can't ask him.'

'No, course you can't. Forget it. It's nothing.'

*

Nothing?

Nothing of the sort. When Dad came home, after Rhiannon had gone, Ginny looked at him differently, trying to imagine him a criminal. She couldn't; there wasn't any crime she could think of that she could see him committing. Then, for the first time in a week, she remembered that social worker, Wendy Stevens, and what the visit had made her worry about. To hear of someone talking about prison in connection with her father wasn't nothing, by any means.

That Monday was her first evening at the Yacht Club, so she didn't eat with him. She'd have something when she came in later, she told him, and set off down the lane. At the parking area by the beach, she turned left and into a field full of tussocky lumps of gorse and marram grass and little sand-filled depressions, just like bunkers on a golf course, which led along beside the estuary as far as the little harbour next to the railway station, where the Yacht Club stood. It was a hot evening, and the sun shone full on the great round hills behind the main road, and the sky above them was a bright pearly blue. Sheep, lazy tattered fat things, moved slowly aside as she wandered past. This warm marine light, this silence . . . they were the emblems of her kingdom. She was at home.

Harry Lime was young and short and thickset, with long-lashed blue eyes. Both he and Angie were ambitious: they wanted to make a name for the restaurant. But that didn't stop them from laughing or being friendly. Angie was short too, and her laughter was of a different kind. She was wittier than Harry, more cynical and shrewd. She was in charge in the kitchen and Harry was in charge in front, and there were a couple of students who waited on the tables, and an elderly lady who worked the dishwasher, and a girl called Gwen, who helped Angie in the kitchen. Ginny's job was to lay tables, fold napkins, make sure the biscuits and the cheese board were stocked up, trim spring onions and celery, top up the salt and pepper, and do any one of a dozen other jobs that Harry or Angie wanted doing. She soon found that she was going to love it. She loved the atmosphere in the kitchen, brisk and clean and hot and busy, full of temperamental cursing and sudden flurries of singing. And she loved the two dining rooms – the front one, cool and open, overlooking the yachts and the river and the little wooden railway bridge, and the smoky little back one where the bar was, with Harry darting this way and that, grinning gap-toothed and tossing olive after olive absentmindedly into his mouth and forever hitching up the trousers that kept slipping under his paunch.

Within half an hour Ginny felt so much at home that she was able to tell them she was going to work at the Dragon as well.

'That bugger Calvert, he's neurotic,' said Harry. 'Don't you think he's neurotic, love?'

'If he wasn't when you started going on about him, then he should be by now,' said Angie, who was stirring some kind of sauce.

'Oh, come on,' said Harry, 'you should hear what he says about this place. It's slanderous, I swear it is. And what's that I saw on the wall there the other day? I was just looking through the window as I went past – has he got paintings hanging up there?'

Painting was Mr Calvert's latest hobby. Ginny felt she ought to defend him, though privately she thought his pictures were terrible.

'He does them himself,' she said. 'They're . . .'

Harry was fascinated. 'He did 'em himself? He does these paintings and hangs 'em up in his own café?'

'He sells them,' Ginny told him. 'They've all got prices on.'

'What? He actually sells 'em? Are they any good?'

'Well . . .'

'Don't lie, girl,' said Angie. 'I can tell.'

'How much does he ask for 'em?' said Harry.

'Forty pounds, fifty pounds, that sort of price.'

Ginny was cutting up French-style loaves into chunks and putting them in little baskets. Harry picked up a piece and absentmindedly started tearing it apart, he was so interested in these paintings of Mr Calvert's.

'And has anyone bought one?' he said, throwing a piece of bread into his mouth.

'I don't know. I'll ask tomorrow.'

'Look at you, you messy pig,' Angie said to him. 'Crumbs all over you. Get out, go and do some work, go on.'

Winking at Ginny and tossing up another piece of bread, Harry Lime went out without the lemon he'd come in for. Angie saw it on the table and asked Ginny to take it through to the bar.

'Silly bugger, he'd forget his trousers if they weren't sewn on,' she said.

When Ginny got back, there was someone else in the kitchen, sitting at the table calmly slicing some carrots into matchstick-sized pieces with quick, accurate taps of a knife.

'Andy!' she said, delighted. 'What're you doing here? Have you left the Castle?'

'I got the sack,' he said. 'It's all right, it's quite fair. I was next on the list. Pass me that dish.'

'What list?' Ginny sat down to fill the salt and pepper mills.

'Carlos, the chef, right, he fires people in strict rotation – first in, first out. Every so often one of his rackets gets busted, and he has to have someone to blame. Someone to take the rap. *Duw annwyl*, you should have seen us last night. We were all in there and he was making *Glühwein*—'

'*Glühwein* in the summer?' said Angie, listening.

'What's *Glühwein*?' said Ginny.

'Oh, you know, mulled wine. You heat it up with spices and stuff and drink it with your après-ski kit. I know it's the wrong drink for the summer, but Carlos is insane, man, he's deranged. He sent me up to the bar for some port, to stiffen it a bit, he says. He had to send to the bar because the boss has put a new lock on the cellar and Carlos hasn't found the key yet, but he will. Anyway, Barry in the bar's drunk, see, so he gives me a bottle of brandy instead. "Brandy for my friend Carlos," he says, "give him brandy." "*Duw*," says Carlos, "look at this, lads, Welsh port – this'll warm your cockles up." There's us all sweating like pigs in there already. He pours it all in – beautiful stuff it was, Rémy Martin or something – and then he takes this poker thing he's been heating in the gas flame. It's red hot, and he bungs it in, and whoosh! The whole lot goes up.

The flames hit the ceiling, Carlos's eyebrows are burnt off, all the waiters are squealing with terror, and then the boss walks in.

' "What's going on? Good God! Good God! What's happened?" he says, and Carlos points the poker at me.

' "This casual staff," he says, "entertainment is all they care about. Swallowing the knives is bad enough, but I will not have fire-eating in my kitchen."

' "Out!" says the boss. "Out! Out!" '

'I don't know how that place is still standing,' said Angie.

'So that was it, see,' Andy went on. 'Still, it was a good laugh. Carlos gave me a whole side of smoked salmon to take away. I had to stuff it down me leg to get it past the porter. Me and Dafydd, we're living on smoked salmon and baked beans now, in the caravan. We're taking it down the beach on Wednesday. You ought to come and pay a visit.'

'I will,' said Ginny.

The last of the sunlight through the open door soaked the whole kitchen in gold, and everything was wonderful. Andy was there, and everything was great.

*

Next morning, in the Dragon, she looked more closely at Mr Calvert's pictures. He was a science fiction fan, and these were science fiction pictures – women in brass corsets fighting huge green lizards, or sunsets on Jupiter with smudgy purple shadows going the wrong way. The colours were so violent and applied so clumsily that Ginny felt uncomfortable looking at them. What was more, she knew from her own efforts that while drawing human beings wasn't easy, if you looked carefully enough and tried hard, you could usually see how bodies fit together. To look at Mr Calvert's paintings, though, you'd have thought it was impossible. They had titles like *Interstellar Alchemy* or *Dragon Dawn*, and Ginny wouldn't have given 10p for the lot; but there they were with little stickers saying forty pounds or fifty pounds. She liked Mr Calvert, so she had to pretend to be impressed.

She had something else on her mind, though, and she didn't want to tell Rhiannon about it. As soon as she finished, which was at twelve o'clock, she slipped away and went down the hill to the station. She was just in time to catch the midday train to Porthafon.

It got there at a quarter to one. The station was next to the harbour, which at one time had been a working place, full of ships taking on cargoes of slate, but now was cluttered with expensive yachts belonging to tourists. Ginny wandered around and sat on a bollard eating some chips and an apple, then she set off to look for Jubilee Terrace.

She didn't know what she was going to say to Rhiannon's sister. She didn't really know whether she was going to call on her at all; she felt nervous, and her heart was beating as if she had stage fright. When she found the house, in a little slaty terrace above the town, she walked past it and down to the end of the terrace before telling herself not to be so weak.

She turned back and rang the doorbell. The narrow garden was neatly kept, with bright geraniums, edging the path, and unlike its neighbours, this house had no net curtains, so Ginny could see how tidy and clean the front room was.

When the door opened, the woman who stood there blinked in the sunlight, shading her eyes, and took a little step backwards in surprise.

'Mrs Meredith?' said Ginny. 'Rhiannon's sister?'

Helen Meredith blew out her cheeks and ran a hand through her dark hair. She knew who Ginny was; she was utterly taken aback.

'Come in,' she said, standing aside in the narrow hall. 'She . . . You must be Ginny. Is that right? God,

I'm sorry to be so . . . It's just a surprise, that's all. She must have told you.'

'Well, she's my friend,' said Ginny.

She stepped inside, and Helen Meredith shut the door. There was a pause, and they both spoke at once, and Ginny said, 'Sorry. You go first.'

'I was going to say would you like some coffee or something?'

'Oh, thanks. Yeah, I would . . .'

She followed the woman into the little kitchen and sat on a stool while Helen filled a kettle and got out some mugs. Everything was so clean that it looked new. Ginny used to think that other people had newer things than she and Dad did, newer carpets, newer curtains and furniture; it took her some time to realize that it was just that she and Dad didn't clean things as often as everyone else. But then they both had better things to do, as he said when she pointed it out.

'I told her not to say anything,' said Helen Meredith. 'I'm embarrassed now.'

She sat down on the other side of the little breakfast bar, and Ginny could see that she was blushing deep pink. She didn't look away or try to hide it, either.

'What did she tell you?' she said.

'She said you'd met my dad, and you wanted to know about me, whether I was adopted.'

Helen Meredith nodded. 'Just being nosy,' she said. 'I'm sorry.'

'Didn't you ask Dad?'

'No. I don't know why. And . . . I thought it was time I got in touch with Rhiannon . . . That seemed to be a way. I don't know . . .'

The kettle boiled, and she got up to make the coffee.

'Oh, by the way, don't call me Mrs Meredith. I'm Helen,' she said, with her back to Ginny.

'Oh. Right.'

She was quite different from Rhiannon, Ginny thought: clearer and more vivid; stronger, perhaps.

Quickly, while Helen's back was still turned, Ginny said, 'Rhiannon said you asked if my father had been in prison.'

'Oh, God,' said Helen.

She brought the mugs over. Her face was screwed up with embarrassment, and deep red. Ginny had never seen a grown-up look so ashamed.

'I didn't want her to,' she said. 'I knew I shouldn't, soon as I said it. Stupid of me. You haven't asked him, have you?'

'What?' Ginny said. 'Course not! He doesn't know I'm here; he doesn't know anything about it.'

'Good. I'm sorry. I shouldn't have listened . . .'

'Listened? Who to?'

'Someone . . . my husband knows. He said that as far as he knew, your dad had . . . been in prison. That's all. It's probably a mistake.'

'But . . . what was he supposed to've done, to get sent to prison?'

'I don't know,' said Helen, looking really unhappy. 'It's probably . . . like I said, it's probably a mistake.'

Ginny sat watching her for a few moments. Helen was toying with a teaspoon, pushing it slowly around like the hand of a clock, not touching her coffee.

'Well, if you know Dad,' Ginny said finally, 'couldn't you ask him?'

'I couldn't. Not yet. I don't know him well enough. Maybe I wouldn't anyway. It's just . . . No.'

'Does your husband know?'

'Benny? He's never here. He wouldn't know.' She sipped her coffee. 'Tell me about your mam,' she said.

Ginny liked the Welsh *mam* better than the English *mum*; it was almost *maman*.

'She came from Haiti,' she said. 'She was an art student, and she met Dad and they fell in love and got married, and I was born, and then she got hepatitis and died. That's all, really. She was called

Anielle. Anielle Baptiste, that was her maiden name.'

'So you never really knew her?'

'No. I've got a picture of her.'

'*Where* did you say she came from?'

'Haiti. Where the zombies come from. Zombies and voodoo. She spoke French and Creole. But I don't know any Creole; there was no one to teach me.'

'You've never been there? Never seen her family?'

'My family too,' Ginny said. 'No, I never have. I don't think Dad would have anything in common with them, really.'

'They'd have you in common,' said Helen.

'Yeah, well . . . Anyway, I get the feeling Dad never got on with them. They just . . . I don't know anything about them, to tell the truth.'

She wished she did. But whenever she'd asked Dad, he'd told her they were a wealthy family from Port-au-Prince, the capital, but that was all he knew.

'We don't talk about her much,' said Ginny. 'It's just me and Dad, really.'

They sat quietly for a while. It was easier now, much easier than Ginny had thought. Helen told her a little about her own background, how she had quarrelled with her father over some boy and how it had got out of control, so that they'd all said more

39

than they'd meant, and how difficult it was to make the first move back. Ginny came away thinking how nice Helen was, how lucky Rhiannon was to have such a sister. Families were strange, to quarrel so bitterly.

Chapter Three
The mobile home

Ginny spent Sunday waiting impatiently for Dad to go out so that she could call Rhiannon and tell her about her visit to Helen. He spent the morning slumped on the sofa reading the paper, as usual, but finally in the afternoon he decided to go and look at a boat he was thinking of buying, and she rushed to the phone at once.

'Rhiannon – guess what? I've been to see your sister!'

'*What*? When?'

'Yesterday. She's great, honestly; she was so nice . . . Her husband wasn't there; she was on her own. The thing about my dad, you know – it was just a rumour she'd heard from someone who knows her husband. Probably a mistake. But I had to go; I couldn't help it . . .'

She sensed that Rhiannon wasn't pleased. It was as if Ginny had somehow stolen Helen for herself; or it might simply have been that her parents were nearby and she couldn't respond with more excitement. She'd have to be tactful, Ginny thought.

In fact, next day in the Dragon, Rhiannon was able to speak more easily, and they spent most of the morning talking intently behind the coffee machine on the counter, analysing everything Ginny could remember about what Helen had said, what the house looked like, what she looked like, what Ginny had said to her.

'You'll have to go and see her,' she told Rhiannon. 'She's really friendly. You'd love her, honest.'

It would have to wait till next weekend, they realized. Maybe they could go together. But no, thought Ginny, be tactful: let Rhiannon meet her sister on her own first. She felt extremely virtuous about that and half wished she could tell Rhiannon and be admired, but that would have spoiled it. Then she realized that too, and laughed.

On Wednesday afternoon, Ginny went down to the beach to help Andy with his mobile home, as he'd taken to calling it.

It was hotter than ever. The car park was full, and there was a line of children waiting to buy ice cream from the two old ladies in the little shop. They sold postcards and cups of tea there as well. The postcards at the front of the rack were all faded, but the ladies left them like that on purpose, to keep the ones at the back nice and bright. Even the ones at the back were getting scratched and dog-eared, though, and they all had rust marks from where the salty air had corroded the rack. The old ladies looked like retired nuns. The tea they sold came not in plastic mugs but in proper cups on a tray. People didn't always bring the cups back, and the two ladies would comb the sand dunes in the evening sunlight, chattering musically, the very souls of sweetness and melancholy.

Ginny sat on the wall by the car park to watch out for Andy and Dafydd, the boy he was going to share the caravan with. She didn't know what Dafydd would be driving; he worked in the garage on the main road, and she'd seen him drive about in dozens of different old cars at one time or another. When at last a car did arrive towing a caravan, she didn't give it more than a glance, because she was sure Dafydd wouldn't be driving a BMW.

But it stopped beside her, and there was Andy in the passenger seat, grinning up at her. She jumped.

'What're you doing in that?' she said. 'That's not Dafydd . . .'

Andy got out. 'This is Stuart,' he said. 'I got another driver. Always wise to have a spare.'

Stuart was leaning across, holding out his hand to shake. Ginny was taken aback; he was about thirty years old and so handsome he was almost unreal, like a model or a film star. At once she felt shy and didn't know what to say, but Andy was completely at ease.

'Well, now, we'll have to back up, driver,' he said. 'Just about a couple of hundred feet, I reckon.'

There were three cars already waiting behind them, unable to pass in the narrow road. Stuart put the BMW in reverse and started to move back, but the other drivers wouldn't budge. Andy went to speak to the first driver. Ginny wondered why Stuart didn't just go on the final hundred feet into the car park and turn around there, but she could see that he and Andy were playing some sort of game, and she settled back to watch it.

Andy was having trouble with the first driver, a brick-faced man with a carful of children.

'What d'you expect me to do? Bloody vertical take-off?' the man was saying heatedly.

'No, no, you could go in the field. Look,' Andy said helpfully, starting to open the gate in the stone wall beside him.

'Why don't *you* go in the field?' roared the driver. He obviously couldn't see that Stuart could have driven straight into the car park. Andy scratched his head, looking doubtful.

'Well, I dunno,' he said. 'The old turning circle's not what it was. I'll have to consult the chauffeur. I say! Carruthers!'

Stuart got out. 'Anything wrong, sir?' he said.

'If this gentleman's kind enough to move back a little way,' Andy called back, 'can we reverse up here and insert the mobile home through this gateway?'

The contrast between Stuart's gleaming BMW and uncanny good looks and the filthy battered old caravan and Andy's scruffiness, not to mention Andy's pretence of picking his nose innocently, was making Ginny giggle. By this time five cars were waiting to get past, and they all had to reverse about ninety feet to let the big BMW back to the gate, and when it got there it wouldn't go in, because no matter how skilfully Stuart reversed it, the caravan was too wide. Andy ran back and forth, pretending to be helpful. At one point he leapt inside the caravan and came out with a twelve-inch ruler, with which he started measuring the width of the gateway. A cry of anger rose from the first car. People started getting out of the vehicles further back, their arms full of towels and beach balls and picnic boxes, leaving the drivers to sort out the mess; and meanwhile Stuart was happily doing whatever

45

Andy told him to do, as Ginny sat on the wall and watched, laughing.

'Why don't you go in the bloody car park and turn round there?' shouted one of the drivers.

'There must be a catch in that,' Andy said. 'What d'you reckon, Gin? Sounds too easy to me.'

'No; do that,' she said.

Stuart nodded, and the BMW surged forward. The caravan door flew wide open with a bang, and a plastic bucket fell out. Andy stood in the middle of the road, nodding wisely.

'See,' he said. 'I told you there was a way of doing it.'

The first car hooted, and Andy jumped aside, taking the bucket with him. The cars in the line followed Stuart into the car park, the drivers scowling and frowning at Andy, who stood holding the bucket like someone collecting for charity. It took less than a minute for Stuart to turn the car around and come out again, facing up the lane. He stopped for Andy and Ginny to get in, and said, 'Where do we go now?'

'Up to the railway bridge,' said Andy. 'We can't get into old Alston's field down here anyway.'

'Well, why did you come all the way down?' Ginny asked.

'To pick you up,' said Stuart.

She was sitting in the front, Andy in the back, and now as she looked at Stuart she felt overcome with shyness again. He must be a film star, she thought; no one could be that handsome and not be famous for it. He had dark curly hair and bright-blue eyes, and his clothes were like his car, expensive and luxurious: soft cream trousers and dark-blue polo shirt. His bare feet on the pedals looked tough and expert.

'What do you do, Ginny?' he said, manoeuvring smoothly past another car.

'Oh, I'm at school,' she said. 'That's all. What about you?'

'I'm a playboy,' he said.

'You know that house by the Yacht Club?' Andy said from the back. 'The one on stilts? Stuart's renting it.'

'Oh, I love that house!' Ginny said.

'You know it, then?' said Stuart.

'Only from the outside.'

'You'll have to come and visit.'

The one-storey wooden house was built like a boat, with railings around a flat roof and portholes instead of windows. When the tide came in, the house stood above the water on its stilts, and a flight of steps led down to where a dinghy was usually tied up. Ginny had loved it from the moment she'd first seen it, but she'd never found out who lived there. Now that Stuart had come to enter her kingdom, though, the least she could do was pay it a state visit.

'Is this where we go?' he said.

He turned the car into the courtyard of the shop by the railway bridge, then waited while Andy opened a gate into the field next to it. They bumped over the tussocky grass to the far corner. There was a hedge that separated it from the caravan site, and in the very centre of the field stood the half-built shell of Mr Alston's house, with piles of bricks and a cement mixer beside it.

'Where d'you want it?' said Stuart.

'This'll do,' said Andy.

They got out, and Andy began to screw down the legs of the caravan.

'Can I look inside?' said Ginny.

'Help yourself,' he said. 'Put the kettle on, that's what you can do. We'll have some coffee.'

It was a shabby, battered old caravan, and worse inside than out, with holes in the hardboard panelling and yellowing tape over a crack in the window and a broken catch that wouldn't hold the cupboard door shut. There were two foam mattresses on the bunks and a couple of sleeping bags lying in a pile of dirty clothes on the floor.

She found a kettle and a plastic container of water and some matches, and lit the gas in the tiny stove, holding the kettle in place while the trailer rocked and shook as they settled it on its legs. When the water boiled, she found some more or less clean mugs and made the coffee. There was no milk, of course, and no sugar, either. When she opened the little kitchen cupboard, a powerful fishy smell came out, and she wrinkled her nose and took a step back before looking more closely. A vast pink slab was lying there sweating.

'What on earth is that thing in the cupboard?' she said, taking two mugs of black coffee outside. Andy and Stuart were sitting on the step, and they moved to make room for her between them.

'Oh, that's me smoked salmon,' said Andy. 'We better finish that off tonight; it's getting a bit vigorous. You fancy a slice now?'

She made a face.

'You not having any coffee?' Stuart said to her.

'I've seen the mugs,' she said.

He looked at his doubtfully but sipped anyway.

'What do you really do?' she said. 'You're not really a playboy, are you? I didn't think they were real.'

'Oh, they are,' he said. 'They play polo, they

gamble, they go skiing and motor racing and jet setting.'

'Not here, though,' she said.

'No; I'm on holiday,' he said. 'All that pleasure, it wears you out. No; really, I'm an anthropologist.'

'A what? Do you go in jungles and things?'

'Not if I can help it. I study religion, magic, witchcraft. I was in Brazil earlier this year. Fascinating.'

'Have you been to Haiti?'

'Yes, I have, actually.'

'My mother came from there.'

'Did she? Do you speak Creole?'

'No. She died when I was only little. I've never been there.'

'It's an amazing place. I spent some time with a voodoo priest, learning all about it.'

'Could you teach me about voodoo?'

'Sure.'

'You ought to do voodoo on Joe Chicago,' she said, turning to Andy.

She felt him tense. He didn't say anything for a moment or two, and Stuart turned to see why.

'Who's Joe Chicago?' he said.

'He's a thug,' said Andy. 'White trash.'

'Why's he called Joe Chicago anyway?' said Ginny.

'That leather jacket he wears, it comes from Chicago,' Andy explained.

'Is that all?'

'It's true!'

'But that's as if I called myself Ginny Korea because of my trainers,' she said.

'Why's he after Andy?' Stuart asked her.

'He won't tell me,' she said.

'You want to stay away from him.' said Andy shortly. 'He's horrible, he's dangerous. Don't have nothing to do with him.'

He wouldn't say any more. Presently Stuart said he had to go and see about renting a boat. 'Come and visit my house,' he said before he drove off. He'd left most of his coffee, Ginny noticed.

'Is he rich?' she said.

'His dad's a millionaire. But he's too busy to spend his money, so Stuart spends it for him.'

'He's nice. I like him.'

Andy had closed his eyes. They sat there in the sun, listening to the shouts of children on the beach or in the sand dunes and the sound of a distant aircraft taking off across the estuary.

'Andy,' she said after a few minutes, 'when you were a kid, did you feel different from everyone else because you were black?'

He didn't answer for such a long time that Ginny eventually prodded his foot with hers.

'I'm thinking,' he said. Then he said, 'I feel different for all sorts of reasons. Being black's one, of course it is. Being adopted's another. Being . . . well, everything else I am. Course I feel different.'

'Do you know who your real parents are?' she asked.

'No, and I don't care, either.'

Ginny couldn't believe that. She said, 'But don't you want to know where they came from and who they were? They might be nice. They might be really glad. You can do that now; I read about it. If you're adopted, you can find out who your parents are.'

'Nice,' he said bitterly. 'Hundred to one, you know what she is, my mother? She's a prostitute. And my father, he'd be one of her customers. Then when I was born she ditched me somewhere and the council shoved me off on them down there.' He nodded toward the south, meaning the town where his adoptive parents lived. 'Nice, you reckon? Bloody rubbish. You think I want to look it all up and find that out? I couldn't care less about her. She just left me, didn't she? To hell with her. I don't want to know. I am what I am. I'm free, see. I got no ties.'

She leaned against the doorframe, watching him. He was gazing down at the grass; she couldn't see the expression in his eyes, but she felt it to be distant and cold.

'Different . . .' he said after another pause. 'I can't go anywhere without being different. I'm not even the same as other black kids. When I was in Bristol, right, doing my catering course, I felt a bloody idiot because these other guys, black guys, they came up to me first day and started talking dialect, patois, you know? Rasta kind a ting, maan? Well, *Duw*, I never felt such a fool in all me life. I couldn't understand a word . . . And what could I say? Sorry, fellers, I can't understand you, I'm Welsh? Ridiculous. Okay, I sound Welsh, but I'm not Welsh . . . Not African, either. I'm just a white kid with a black face, that's what I am. Don't belong anywhere.'

'Right!' Ginny said. 'That's just what I feel, exactly what I feel!'

'You're all right anyway. When you draw pictures, it doesn't matter what colour you are.'

'Ah, no,' Ginny said. 'That's not true. I think it *does* matter. I think there might be a difference between the way white people paint and the way black people do. Just as there's a difference between French paintings and Chinese paintings . . . You can see it.'

'What is it, then? What's the difference between black art and white art?'

'That's what I don't know, you see! That's the point! That's why I said I feel like you, I don't know where I belong . . .'

'Right. So you're free, then, ain't you?'

'Free?'

'Free to do anything. Like me. I don't know where I belong, so I'm free. No one's got a hold on me.'

Except Joe Chicago, thought Ginny. But he wouldn't tell her anything about that. And it was more difficult than she'd said, more difficult than she could explain. After a while they went and bought some ice cream from the two old ladies and looked on the beach for crabs, but the crabs must have been hiding, because they didn't find a single one.

Ginny was good at drawing; everybody said so. The teachers would soon find out how good her pictures were and put them on the display board. At one school she tried drawing badly on purpose, but they still praised her and still pinned up her pictures. Then she saw how stupid they were at that school, and hated them for it, and grew so unhappy she could hardly breathe.

That was the place where they lived in a basement. Dad slept in the sitting room and she had the only bedroom. The stove and the fridge and the kitchen sink were all in the sitting room too. There was a little boy who lived upstairs. They used to play in the yard together, but he was always crying. He got scratched by a cat once and had to be taken upstairs to lie down. When they'd taken him up, Ginny stayed in the yard alone, making a town for her plastic rabbit to live in among the flowerpots behind the big coal bin, wondering if the little boy would die from the cat scratch.

In another school she had to wear a dark-green uniform with a straw hat held on by a tight elastic band under her chin. The playground was two streets away, and they walked there in pairs, each girl holding her neighbour's hand. Ginny had to walk with a girl called Jackie. Jackie kept letting go of her hand, until the teacher saw and told her off.

Ginny had a photograph of her mother in a leather frame, which always stood beside her bed. Everyone said how alike they looked. Her mother was called Maman, which was French. Ginny spoke to Maman every night, asking her to ask the Virgin Mary to send some angels to guard her against bad dreams. Once some girls wanted to tell her a secret, and so that she wouldn't give it away, they made her swear on her mother's deathbed. She was very frightened. She thought about it that night and couldn't get it out of her mind. She imagined a deathbed as a special sort of bed which was delivered to the house when it was time for you to die, and you'd know, everybody would know, and slowly it would get closer to bedtime and you wouldn't want to go to bed, but you must, you had to, it was time. What happened on the deathbed was too horrible to think of. She lay rigid

that night, and when Dad came in to kiss her, as
he always did before he went to bed, he found her
pillow drenched with tears. She couldn't explain it
at all.

Chapter Four
A phone call

Just as Ginny was leaving next morning to go to the Dragon, the phone rang. She recognized the caller's voice at once and found her heart thumping, because it was Wendy Stevens.

'Hello, Ginny! Is your dad in?'

'No, he's at work. D'you want his number? He's probably in the office—'

'I've got his work number, thanks, love. I thought he'd be at home, for some reason.'

'Oh. Well . . .'

'Don't go. Are you busy?'

'Well, I've got a job to go to, I've got to be there in half an hour, but . . .'

'A job? What're you doing, then?'

'In a café. Nothing special.'

'Nice. Listen . . . Did your dad say anything the other day after I left?'

'What, about you?'

'Yes. About why I came.'

Now her knees were trembling. Ginny sat down on the floor and steadied her elbow against the wall.

'No,' she said.

'He didn't tell you about what's happening in Liverpool?'

'Liverpool . . . I don't know what you mean. What *is* happening?'

'Well . . . Oh, look, let me ring him now. He'll tell you himself; it's better.'

'No! Wait! What is it? *Please* tell me! I asked him about you the other day, but he wouldn't say anything. I *knew* there was something wrong. But if you're thinking what I think you are, it's not true, it's a lie, I swear it.'

There was a silence then for a second or two.

'What d'you mean, love?' said Wendy Stevens, in a different voice. 'What do you think I'm thinking?'

'About . . . You're investigating him, aren't you? Isn't that it?'

'Investigating him? Whatever for?'

Now it was Ginny's turn to pause.

'I thought someone might've – you know – might have told you something that wasn't true. About him and me. You know, like you read in the papers, when they take kids into care. That's why I thought you'd come, you see. I was afraid . . .'

'Let me get this straight. You thought I was checking up on whether your father was abusing you? Is that what you mean?'

'Yeah.' Ginny felt breathless. 'Yeah, that's it. And if it wasn't that . . . well, us being different races. I know they don't like white parents having black kids. So I thought maybe it might be that . . . I don't know.'

'That's only a guideline, and it only applies to adoption or fostering, and you're not adopted or fostered, you're his child, so forget that. As for the other thing – *is* he abusing you?'

'No! God, no! Course not!'

'I never thought he was. It wasn't that at all. But you mean you've been thinking this all the time? Didn't you ask him about it? Actually, no, it wouldn't be easy, would it?'

She was sounding far more straightforward and sensible than she had the other day. Maybe it was because Ginny couldn't see her smiling all the time; or maybe she wasn't smiling now.

'Well, what is it about, then?' Ginny said, worried differently but no less worried.

'That's why I need to talk to him. I don't think I ought to tell you like this, over the phone.'

'But you can't leave it like this! I won't see him till nine o'clock, probably; he's working late . . . You're not going to split us up? You're not going to take me away?'

She knew she sounded distressed, but she

couldn't help it; she genuinely didn't know what powers they had.

'No,' said Wendy Stevens. 'No one could do that. No one wants to do that, even if they could.'

'Then what's it about? Is it about my mother? Is she alive or something?'

That was a shot in the dark: about the wildest thing Ginny could think of. Wendy Stevens hesitated again.

'What do you know about your mother?' she said.

'Only what he's told me. She died soon after I was born.'

'Ah,' she said. 'Right. Well, listen, Ginny. What's going on concerns your dad, but not in a bad way, not in any way that'll split your family up or anything of that sort. But *he's* going to have to tell you what it is; I can't. It wouldn't be right. What I'll do is I'll ring him now at work and tell him what's going on, so he'll know, and I'll tell him what we've said this morning—'

'Don't tell him what I was worried about!'

'The abuse business?'

'Yeah. Don't tell him that, *please*. I don't want him thinking . . . Just tell him I was worried, OK?'

'I understand. And listen, Ginny . . . I'll be coming down again in a couple of days. We'll have a talk then, if you like.'

'Oh . . . right. Why are you coming down?'

'That's what he'll have to tell you. You better get off to your job now; you'll be late.'

'Yeah . . . Thanks.'

'Ta-ra, Ginny.'

The phone receiver buzzed in Ginny's hand. She stood up slowly and replaced it.

She had a lot to tell Rhiannon and no time to tell her in; the Dragon was busier than at any time she'd known it, and what with serving coffee, clearing dirty cups away, selling doughnuts and scones and pieces of Mrs Calvert's home-made cake, and trying to get the tables clear and set up for lunch with their salt and pepper shakers and sugar packets and plastic ketchup bottles, she hadn't managed to exchange two words with her friend all morning.

And since Rhiannon was going shopping with her mother that afternoon, there wouldn't be time then, either. So Ginny came away frustrated and spent the afternoon drawing the neighbour's cat, which liked to sleep on their garden wall; and then she went to the Yacht Club and did her job and got more and more tense, waiting to hear what Dad would tell her.

He was in the garden when she came home, lying in the hammock with a can of lager, playing an old

Paul Simon tape on his Walkman. Ginny could hear it: he had it far too loud.

He saw her coming and took it off. She sat down in the deckchair, facing him.

'Dad? Did Wendy Stevens phone you?'

'Yup. She told me you'd spoken.'

He must have had a few lagers already, because he was speaking very carefully and more slowly than usual.

'She said you'd tell me what it was about,' she said.

'Yes. She's right. I didn't like her at first, but I think she's OK, probably. It's very difficult.'

She didn't know what he meant by that, because he said it in the same tone as the rest; he might have meant that it was difficult for her or difficult for him. She waited.

'Ginny, love, she said you were worried they were going to take you away or something. Is that right?'

'Yeah. 'Cause no one said what it was about. I thought they could do that if they wanted to . . . 'Cause they do that, don't they? They take black kids away from white families?'

'Well, they can't. No way. There's no question of that. This is something else entirely. Ginny . . . you've got a brother.'

A *brother?*

63

Silence. She had no idea, absolutely not the slightest notion, of what to say next. He was watching her with careful eyes.

'He's not a child of Maman,' he said after a few moments. 'He's your half-brother. I met ... his mother before I met Maman, you see. Now what's happened, what this is all about, is that his mother has been ill, very ill. She's been looking after him on her own. Like me and you. But she's got cancer, and she's going to die any day. I didn't expect ... I didn't ... Anyway. She's in hospital. She might die tonight, next week, next month, who knows. Robert – that's the boy – he's in care for the moment, but he's going to need a home. So the only place for him is here, you see. That's why Wendy Stevens came the other ... whenever it was ... last week. I didn't tell you then because his mother was going to have an operation. It might have been all right, and then everything would've gone back to normal, and nothing ... no one would've ... I don't know. But unfortunately it wasn't good news. She's very ill. And ... obviously the poor kid, the boy, Robert, he's got to come here.'

He tilted the can of lager back. It was nearly empty. Ginny looked down at her hands, her dark-brown hands, twisted in her lap.

'Is he black?' she asked. 'Was she black?'

'No.'

Perhaps it wasn't a good question. Too bad: too late.

'When's he coming?'

'In a week or so. There'll be a funeral. Well, good God . . . I mean, there could be a miracle; that's what God's supposed to do; she could get better. But I don't suppose she will. So after . . . Whenever she dies. Sometime . . . soon.'

A brother, she thought. A white brother. This was the strangest news she'd ever had. Not even Rhiannon's sister was such strange news as this. Rhiannon would understand part of it but not the rest; only Andy would understand the rest. Because she'd be more isolated now. White brother, white father, black sister. Talk about a sore thumb!

'How old is he?' she said.

'He's a bit older than you.'

'A bit? How much?'

'I can't remember. A few months.'

'Is he the little boy that got scratched by the cat?'

'Scratched by the cat . . . I don't know, love; you must be thinking of someone else. You've never seen him, I do know that.'

'Did you . . . When did you . . . I mean, when you married Maman, did you . . .'

'As soon as I met Maman, I forgot everyone else.

She was the only one. Ginny, I've been stupid not telling you before. I'm sorry to do this to you. I'm not very good at . . . I'll never love anyone more than you, chick. I . . . What I'm trying to say is . . . things are going to change. I can't let the boy grow up in some home somewhere. I'm responsible. You're not responsible, but you're going to have to . . . share the burden. It's not going to be easy. I'm just apologizing. Not your responsibility, but you're stuck with it. It's not fair to you.'

He stopped. His eyes were shut. Ginny felt all kinds of emotions – bewilderment, anger, jealousy, incredulity, excitement, apprehension, even glee – turning over and over inside her like clothes in the tumble dryer. She watched them, but she wasn't connected to them. Perhaps they were feelings she thought she ought to be experiencing rather than those she was; it was too puzzling to tell.

'Robert,' she said.

'That's right. His mother's choice of name.'

'What was she called?'

'Janet.'

'Have you . . . What does he . . . Have you ever seen him?'

'Never. He'll be as new to me as he is to you. But I'm going to go up to Liverpool first, see him, maybe see Janet. Sort things out.'

'Where's he going to sleep?'

There were only two bedrooms. It was a small house, but it had never felt small till now.

He sighed. 'There's a lot of adjustments to be made. I don't know. Probably the office. I'll move all that stuff into my room. We'll manage.'

The office, Ginny realized for the first time, was actually another bedroom. So it was really a three-bedroom house after all.

'Will he go to the school?'

'Yup. I suppose so. Well, yes, he will. I'll have to see the head – what's his name – Bill Evans.'

'He'll have to learn Welsh.'

'You'll have to help him.'

Ginny said nothing. There was a long silence. He reached down from the hammock and squeezed her hand, and she nodded.

'Yeah,' she said finally. 'Right. Wow.'

The best time ever in her life was a bright sunny morning with the wind chasing fat white clouds through the blue sky, and there was a lady pinning out sheets on the line, and they billowed like the clouds, big fresh-smelling moist clouds that swelled and flapped and swung up high. The lady was singing, and the song thrilled through the clouds and the sheets and filled the immense beaming sky, and Ginny felt that she was so light that she, too, could swing up and be blown along in the wild blue splendour and then there was Dad, and it came true, she was flying, up she went onto his shoulders, over the sheets, up with the wind in the song and the clouds and the endless dazzling sky, and she beat on his head for joy in a world of snowy-white sheets and billowing clouds and the immortal wide intensity of blue.

Chapter Five
Gwynant

The first thing Ginny wanted to do was tell Rhiannon. They spent the morning talking closely together by the coffee machine; behind its steamy fragrant shelter they felt that secrets were safe. More than one customer had to cough loudly and tap on the counter to be noticed that morning.

In the afternoon they took their bikes and rode up the Gwynant valley. The river that entered the sea so widely and placidly in the Yacht Club estuary had a quite different character in the hills: it was narrow, sparkling bright, and icy cold, splashing and tumbling over ancient grey granite and falling in cascades through mossy oakwoods. Ginny and Rhiannon toiled up the twisting road with the sun beating off the rocks beside them until they reached a narrow bridge over the river, where there was a slow-swirling pool to swim in.

Cold as the water was, they plunged in at once. It didn't take long, in that icy brightness, to cool down; after five minutes they climbed out and lay dripping on the hot lichen-patterned rock. A great sloping shelf of it had split hundreds of years before into clumsy rectangular blocks as big as cars, and smaller blocks lay tumbled and confused in the river itself. The water rushed smoothly between them and splashed into whiteness below. You could get to the other side of the river in three jumps, or steps, if your legs were long enough.

They lay there saying nothing, feeling the cold on their skins gradually melt into heat and listening to the endless splash of the water and the scraping of the insects in the grass.

'So,' Rhiannon said eventually. 'Robert, eh?'

'Yeah. What'm I going to *do*?'

'I'm giving it the best of my attention,' said Rhiannon lazily. 'I shall come to a conclusion shortly. Be patient.'

'You discover a sister, and I discover a brother. Isn't it crazy? At least your sister's all right.'

'I can't say much for her husband, though.'

'What? You've met him?'

'Aha. I went there last night. Didn't I tell you?'

Ginny propped herself up on her elbows. Rhiannon was smirking, but Ginny didn't mind; it relieved her of the guilt of having stolen the first visit.

'What happened?' she said.

'Oh, I told Mam I was going out with Peter, and

she thought great, 'cause she likes Peter. But I just went on the train and rang the doorbell, and that was it. Her husband was there. He's a *creep*. My brother-in-law. *Ach y fi.* He was wearing a business suit and business shoes, and he had a neat little black business moustache. *Duw*, you'd think he was a young executive, and all he does is sell double glazing. Wow, what a prune. I don't know why she married him, I really don't.'

Ginny tried to imagine the warm, vivid person she'd met the other day in love with a neat little man with a black moustache.

'So what did you talk about?' she said.

'Well, it was so strange, you can imagine: this grown-up woman looking like me and – d'you think she looks like me? Do I look like her?'

'Yeah . . . She's not as droopy as you.'

'What d'you mean? I'm not droopy.'

'Bendy, then.'

'*Bendy*,' repeated Rhiannon with utter contempt. 'Graceful, that's what you're trying to say. So she's not as graceful as me. Well, fair enough.'

'But what did you *say*?'

'I was coming to that. It was, oh, how's Mam and Dad, do they ever talk about me? She said that a couple of times. I couldn't say no, could I? So I said yeah, they did sometimes. I told her about the

Dragon. They didn't have that when she left; see, Dad was an engineer on the airfield.'

'I didn't know that.'

'Well, he was. She said she couldn't imagine him running a café, and I said he doesn't, Mam and I do. And she wanted to know about me, you know, all school and dull stuff like that. And bloody Benny sitting there listening, suspicious, checking me out. I mentioned you, right, I said you'd told me you'd seen her, and her face went red all at once. She shook her head, just a tiny bit, so he couldn't see, and she went—'

Rhiannon mouthed *No* and looked frightened. She was a good actress; Ginny could see it exactly.

'Because of him?' she said.

'Yeah. She didn't want him to know. She *does* fancy your dad; I could tell. And later on, when I had to go, she came down into town with me, and then she could talk more easily. Benny's so jealous, he's jealous of everything. He knows that Helen knows your dad, but he thinks it's only because your dad was setting up some computer thing in the office she works in, this architect's place. That's all. If he thought there was anything else, I don't know what he'd do. I *think* she's seen your dad since, maybe they had lunch together, something like that, went for a drink or something. But I tell you – you know the thing about your dad being in prison? You know where that came from?'

'What? Where?'

'Benny told her, 'cause obviously he was jealous, he wanted to put her off. But *he* heard it from that Joe Chicago you told me about!'

Ginny blinked. 'Get off,' she said. 'How would Benny know Joe Chicago? He comes from Aberystwyth. That's miles away.'

'Ah, that's it; he doesn't. He lives in Porthafon,' Helen said. 'And he knows Benny because . . . I can't remember. He just does. But he was the one it came from.'

'Stupid!' said Ginny, rolling over on her back. 'That's impossible. Joe Chicago has nothing to do with my dad.'

'Well, Helen said Joe had been in jail, see, and he knew your dad because that was where they met.'

Ginny scoffed. She'd never heard anything so hopeless in her life. High up in the profound blue above her, an aircraft like a little silver speck was leaving a condensation trail of pure white. The aircraft was too far away to hear, but up there somewhere was a lark, trilling and carolling like an angel. She could see the aeroplane but not hear it, hear the lark but not see it, and the two things came together in her mind, a plane that sang like a bird.

Sleepy, warm, and moved to an incomprehensible happiness by the blue and the white and the singing, she dismissed the fantastic nonsense about jail and gangsters and double glazing salesmen and gave herself up to the sun.

Rhiannon was saying something. Ginny murmured, 'What?'

'I said it looked as if it was stuck on. His moustache. Part of a kit, probably. The young executive kit. He probably washes it overnight and leaves it on the edge of the bath. I bet he's got a pretend car phone too; they always have. He probably pretends to be speaking into it while he's waiting at traffic lights. What d'you reckon it's like, kissing a moustache?'

Ginny came a little more awake now. In all her life, she was certain, the only male kiss she'd ever received had been from her father. Here was that question again, awake in the darkness: Who would kiss her if she was a different colour? But she had to answer.

She said, 'Like nuzzling a carpet.'

'You know what the Victorians said? I read it in the *Daily Mail*. They said kissing a man without a moustache is like eating an egg without salt!'

That seemed so funny that Ginny burst out laughing. 'Eating an egg without . . . Oh, *Duw*, that's amazing! Eating a man without salt is like kissing an egg without a moustache!'

Rhiannon was giggling too. 'Kissing a moustache without salt is like eating a man without an egg . . .'

Now they were helpless, rolling about on the bumpy rock aching with laughter. On and on it went, getting crazier and crazier, and the dark question turned around and retreated back into the dimness it lived in. Still awake, though; not asleep.

Later on they jumped across the river and into the little grove of trees below the bridge. They were oak trees, gnarled and bent and hardly any higher than the stone wall that ran along the road above. Ginny felt that they were very ancient, these trees. Under their shade it was quiet and still, and the moss-covered rocks, flecked and dappled with sunlight, seemed like hassocks in a ruined church. She supposed that the Druids would have come to places like this to worship their gods.

Ginny said, 'Did she know who you were when she came to the door?'

'Who, Helen? Not for a few seconds. After all, I was six or something when she left. I'm bound to look different. I've got bosoms, for a start. I keep trying to bring them to Peter's attention.'

'Doesn't he notice?' said Ginny.

'He's too nice. He's kind. The trouble with kind

people is they're not sexy. Maybe I'll ask Helen about it. She's bound to know the answer to life. Worldly wise, that's what she is. Bound to be.'

'Maybe it's worth having a kind person, even if they're not sexy,' Ginny said, plucking shreds of moss from the rock she was sitting on.

'No,' said Rhiannon, sighing. 'It's funny, isn't it. Sexy people couldn't care less if they're kind or not, but all the kind people'd love to be sexy. The trouble is, you're either one or the other.'

'I bet some people are both.'

'Impossible. It's tragic. Life's a tragedy, see.'

'Oh, right,' said Ginny.

She threw some moss at Rhiannon and hit her on the nose.

'Get off,' said Rhiannon wearily.

'Why's this bridge newer than the rest of the road?' said Ginny.

'It's the broken bridge. Pont Doredig.'

'Pont Doredig . . . Le Pont Cassé. Why's it broken?'

'Well, it's mended now, stupid. There was some accident here, some story about a car. I don't know . . . a long time back.'

Ginny looked up at the bridge. It was narrow, with room for only one car to cross at a time, and the stonework was newer than the old dry-stone wall that bordered the road. She tried to imagine a car crashing through and into the river, but perhaps that wasn't what had happened . . .

'What did your dad say about Robert?' said Rhiannon.

'I told you.'

'Tell me again. I want to work it out exactly. *How* old did he say he was?'

So they went through it again, and crossed back to the rock where their towels were, and drank some of the cold pure water from the river by lying down like lions and dipping their faces into the flow; and then they gathered their things and freewheeled back down the valley, hardly having to pedal at all. They went over and over what Dad had said, but there was no more in it than there had been before, and Robert was still a mystery. Ginny knew what she felt now; she felt apprehensive. A sister living twenty miles away, a grown-up sister with a house and a job and worldly wisdom, was a piece of good fortune; but an unseen brother your own age who was going to invade your own home was a threat.

Once she visited her Grandma and Grandad. The house was very quiet, and Ginny had to tiptoe across the shiny wooden floor in her slippers. If she stood on the rug and slid one foot toward the other, the rug came up in a straight ridge between them, but she mustn't do that; the rug wasn't made for that.

She heard Grandad and Grandma whispering together once in the kitchen while she stood outside, and through the frosty glass door she saw Grandma hit Grandad and heard him say, 'Hush, quiet, for God's sake,' in a loud, shaky whisper, and then he turned away, holding his arm.

There were old books in the living room. She was allowed to read books if she sat on the sofa with them. Sitting on the floor wasn't allowed: we don't sit on floors in this house, we don't have dirty little girls who sit on floors in this house, we don't read books on the floor. Ginny sat with her book on the sofa in the endless cold silence that smelled of furniture polish, the silence that was sliced into regular little pieces by the tick of the tall clock behind the door.

Grandad kept licking his lips. His eyes were the same colour as the blue in the curtains, and they didn't look at you, they looked sideways past you. When he turned the page of a magazine he licked his forefinger and pressed it on the page, squeezing up the corner between his thumb and his wet finger just the way Ginny had done with the rug in the hall.

Chapter Six
The ghost train

At breakfast time on Saturday, Wendy Stevens phoned again, and Dad came back into the kitchen after taking the call and said, 'Well, that's it, love. I've got to go to Liverpool, sort things out.'

'Has she died?'

'Yes. Last night. Damn it, I should have gone yesterday, I knew I should. But she wouldn't have known . . .'

He sat down and pushed his cereal away. Ginny watched him carefully. His mouth was tight, and his eyes weren't looking; they were focused on something a long way away.

'Did you love her?' Ginny said.

'Well, it's complicated; you can't tidy things up in a sentence or two . . . Sorry, love, I'm just thinking about it – it's all rather mixed up. D'you want to come to Liverpool? I'll only be going to see the hospital and the undertaker, I suppose, that kind of thing. Wendy Stevens. See the boy too. Poor kid. It won't be very interesting, but come if you like.'

'No! I can't! I'm working . . . I mean, they're

expecting me, I can't let them down . . . Anyway, I'd be in the way.'

'Well, you wouldn't, but OK. I don't know when I'll be back. You'll be all right?'

'Will you be bringing him back?'

'No, no, not today. No, he'll stay there till the funeral . . . next week sometime.'

'What about Grandad and Grandma? Couldn't they have him?'

She heard the urgency in her voice. She hadn't meant to sound like that, but everything was more urgent now that it was settled and there was no last-minute hope that she'd get better.

'No. Impossible.'

'Why do we never see them, Dad? It's as if they're dead or something. They looked after me once, didn't they?'

'I can't stop and talk about it now, love. Sorry. But they're out of the question. I'll tell you more later – I've got to move.'

He bent and gave her a scratchy kiss, and then he was gone. A couple of minutes later, she heard the throaty rasp of the car starting and driving away up the lane towards the main road.

Rhiannon was full of sympathy, but it wasn't for her; it was for the mysterious Robert.

'Imagine it,' she said, her beautiful eyes practically melting with tears. 'He's lived all his life with his mam and he doesn't know anyone else, and she gets cancer and dies. Then he has to leave his home and go and live with strangers. It must be terrible for him.'

Ginny was silent and a little ashamed. In fact, she thought, she was a lot ashamed, because she simply hadn't considered that aspect of it at all.

'Yeah,' she said. 'I wish I knew what he was like. I wish I knew more about this woman – I mean, his mother. And my grandparents too. It's weird, you know. I remember staying with them once when I was a kid, but I never saw them again. They never write or anything. And he never talks about them.'

'Probably like Helen and my parents: they probably had a steaming row, and they're both too proud to make up,' said Rhiannon. 'I bet you.'

'But how could he *do* that? I mean, how could he have a child with one woman and then go off and marry another one and never mention the first one? All this time I thought I was the only child, and then suddenly, bang, there's another one . . . How could he *do* it?'

'Ah, well, your dad's just sexy.'

'You reckon?'

'Take my word for it.'

'I'll tell him—'

'I'll kill you. Don't you dare.'

Ginny wondered if that meant, according to Rhiannon's theory, that Dad couldn't be kind as well. But she knew it was too simple; things were more complicated than that.

That afternoon, she went to see Andy. When she arrived at the trailer, she found him spraying himself with aftershave lotion so pungent that it defeated even the reek of baked beans and smoked salmon.

'What're you putting that on for?' she said.

'You like it?'

'It's *horrible!* I'd rather smell sweat; I'd rather smell dirty socks, even!'

'Ah, well, they'll know I'm there anyway. You coming to the fair?'

'Is it on? Today? Brilliant!'

'Dafydd's got the car working. You're just in time – how about that. Who's a lucky little Ginny, then?'

He patted her cheeks with his aftershave-laden hands.

'*Ach,*' she said, slapping at him but secretly delighted.

Dafydd was a big, slow, sweet-natured boy of twenty or so. He had long black hair, like a heavy-metal freak, and strong, oil-stained hands that could do anything with machinery. When Ginny was much younger she'd fallen off her bike and twisted the handlebars. She'd hauled it tearfully to the garage on the main road, hoping they could mend it before Dad came home, and it was Dafydd who'd gently listened to her and taken the battered little bike and set the front wheel between his knees and twisted the handlebars till they were straight again. Better still, he'd shown her how to do it too. She'd fallen in love with him on the spot, but he was thirteen and she was nine, and so he was all but grown up and out of reach.

Later he'd passed on to her the comics he loved to read, and they'd shared such delights as *Tank Girl* and *Halo Jones* and *Watchmen* and *Raw* and, best of all, *Love and Rockets*. When she looked at comics she felt a strange knowledge growing inside her, a mixture of excitement and certainty, and she copied the artwork until she could draw Batman and Superman and El Borbah and Maggie and Hopey and Tonantzín, all the classics, almost as well as the originals. Dafydd admired that as much as she admired his skill with engines, but he was still four years older; sixteen and twenty were almost as far apart as nine and thirteen. Besides, she thought now, with Rhiannon's worldly wisdom, he was a kind person; Andy was the sexy one.

'You coming to the fair, then?' Dafydd said, emerging from the bonnet of his ancient MG, parked out of sight behind the trailer.

'Yeah! Great! I didn't know it was on,' she said. 'Is there room for me?'

'You're skinny,' said Andy, patting her bottom. 'Fold your little drumsticks up and get in the back. Go on.'

She did, and with Andy sitting like a lord in front of her, Dafydd got the engine going at the third attempt and they bumped off over the grass and through the gate.

The road along the coast was busy. There wasn't much of a bus service, which was why people used the train, but there was talk of the train service being cut; in which case everyone would have to have a car, Ginny thought, and pump more carbon dioxide into the ozone layer, or whatever it was.

In the meantime, she loved sitting in the back of Dafydd's fume-belching MG and listening to the boys talk. The wind rushed past her face, and the engine roared, and everything was fun.

As they went below the Castle Hotel, Andy said, 'Duck, lads, this is Carlos's day for practising his golf.'

'Does he still have putting competitions on the roof?' said Dafydd.

'No, he's taken up driving now. He uses hard-boiled eggs,' Andy said quite seriously.

'I don't believe in Carlos! I think you're making him up,' said Ginny.

'No, it's true!' said Andy. 'There's this little lad from Wrexham, on some training scheme – Carlos calls him Polka Dot cause of all his spots, right. Anyway, he says to him one day, Boil me up fifty eggs, Polka Dot, give 'em ten minutes, not a second less. So Polka Dot thinks he's going to be let into some Cordon Bleu secret, and he counts out the eggs, one two three four fifty, boils 'em all for ten minutes. Now go up on the roof, says Carlos, taking a practice swing with a ladle, set 'em all up on the edge a foot apart, facing out to sea. Well, Polka Dot's mystified, but Carlos is The Man, you don't argue with The Man, and up goes little Polka Dot with this plastic bowl full of eggs, and taps 'em all on the end and sets 'em all up along the edge. Carlos goes up with his clubs and flies into a passion. You fool! he says. Whoever heard of pointed golf balls, you've got 'em on the wrong end, turn 'em over, turn 'em over! So Polka Dot has to crawl along, turning 'em all the other way up, only he's so nervous he drops half of 'em into the flowerbed below, and Carlos makes him go and pick 'em up and make a salad out of 'em. Mustn't waste food, he says, first duty of a good chef.'

'Oh, go on, it's not true,' said Ginny, but she felt as happy as if it had been.

Dafydd parked the car in a side street, and they swaggered into the harbour car park, where the fair had set up. The smell of hot dogs, the crash of amplified rock and roll, the hum of electricity filled the air. The best time to come was after dark, but any time was good. They went on the Flying Jets and the Dodgem Cars, and Andy put his arm around her shoulders while she drove and crashed and spun; they climbed the rickety old Helter-Skelter and stood at the top, making it sway from side to side, till the owner yelled up to quit it and get on down; they shied at coconuts and got none, they shot at ping-pong balls on jets of water and Dafydd won a teddy bear, they played the arcade games in the tent; and there they came face to face with Joe Chicago.

Ginny was playing a pinball game, with Andy banging the table for her, when suddenly he fell silent. Ginny felt a rush of fear and looked up, and there was Joe Chicago not two feet away, staring at Andy with bleak hot eyes.

He was big, but his bulk looked like muscle, not fat. Lank strands of sandy hair seemed pasted to his greasy head. The famous leather jacket was open, and she saw a thick fur lining and thought how hot he must be, but he seemed as cold as ice.

She felt a hand on her arm: Dafydd, tugging her gently away. She went with him and left Andy there, seemingly at his ease, talking expansively to Joe Chicago as if they were the best of friends.

'What's he want?' said Ginny. 'Why's he after Andy?'

''Cause Andy's a bloody fool,' said Dafydd. 'He gets mixed up in things and he doesn't know how to get out of it. You keep away from that guy; let Andy sort it out.'

She stood by Dafydd while he played a machine that picked up sweets with a crane and dropped them into a tray. He managed to get two, his deft oil-stained hands working their usual charm over machinery, but Ginny kept her eyes on Andy, and she saw Joe Chicago suddenly, without warning, punch Andy hard on the upper arm, a vicious blow that knocked him sideways a couple of feet. She gasped, but Andy didn't seem at all worried, and no one else appeared to have noticed. Ginny was breathless. Without showing the least sign of surprise or alarm, Andy took a couple of ten-pound notes from his pocket and handed them to Joe

Chicago, who nodded and strolled away without looking back.

The whole scene lasted hardly more than a few seconds, but the strange atmosphere between Joe and Andy left Ginny weak. She suddenly seemed to have looked into a pit of dark and strange behaviour of which that punch was only a symbol, a pit that had opened for a moment and then closed again, leaving the sunny surface of the world shadowy and insubstantial.

'Here, have it,' said Dafydd, pushing a toffee into her hand.

'But did you see—'

'Let Andy sort it out,' he said again. 'Don't worry about him. He's got more lives than a cat. Talking of cats, let's have a hot dog . . .'

Two minutes later they were all eating soggy hot dogs dripping with grease and ketchup.

'Boiled onions,' said Andy in disgust. 'I ask you. I should've brought Gertie along – we could have had a slice off her.'

'Who's Gertie?'

'That bloody smoked salmon,' said Dafydd. 'Honest, I'm going to sling it out. I'm fed up with it.'

'She's just getting ripe,' said Andy.

'It lies there singing in the dark,' said Dafydd. 'It's

going to climb out the cupboard and kiss me one of these nights. Aye, aye, look, here's a Ghost Train . . .'

They'd missed it the first time round. Of all the fairground rides, Ginny loved the Ghost Train best of all, and this looked like a good one, the ghosts howling and clanking away inside and Freddy Krueger brandishing his iron fingernails on the front.

Andy wouldn't go on it; he said he was too highly strung. Ginny scoffed and got into the nearest carriage with Dafydd, who paid, and then the siren howled and off they went, bashing through the double doors into the raucous darkness.

Skeletons leapt out, phantoms gibbered, ghouls gnawed corpses, and evil banshees wailed; it was the best Ghost Train Ginny had ever been on. But suddenly everything stopped. The carriage lurched to a halt, the light on the nearest coffin went out, and the distant thud of the generator faltered and died.

They sat in the darkness and silence.

'What's going on?' said Ginny.

'The generator's packed up,' said Dafydd. 'We'll be here for ever. What it is, they need some more ghosts, probably. Just our luck.'

Someone called from outside. 'Don't move! We'll get the power back on in a minute!'

From somewhere ahead in the darkness, a muffled voice said, 'Can't we walk out?'

'No! Stay there! Stay in the carriage!'

Then it was silent again. Outside there was all the noise of the rest of the fair, but it only made the silence in the Ghost Train deeper. Dafydd lit a cigarette, and the glow of light and the smoke around his face made him look like a god in a mysterious temple, surrounded by incense.

'Dafydd?' said Ginny after a while.

'Yeah?'

They were speaking quietly, almost whispering.

'Is Andy in trouble?'

'No more than usual. Just let him be, I would.'

'Has Joe Chicago been in jail?'

'Well, that's what they say. I wouldn't know, myself.'

They sat in silence for a few moments. Then she thought of something else.

'Dafydd, you know Pont Doredig?'

'Oh, the broken bridge, aye. Up Gwynant. I used to go swimming up there.'

'What happened to the bridge? Why's it broken?'

'Oh, that was years ago. This bloke was driving up there one night with his kid in the car, only a baby, and it was a winter night with snow all over the place. I don't know exactly what happened, whether he skidded or went through the wall or something, but anyway he had to leave the car there and go for help. He left the kid there, in the car, wrapped up in this fur-lined jacket, sheepskin, I suppose, to keep it warm. When he got back from the nearest farmhouse or the phone box or whatever, the jacket was gone, stolen, and the kid was dead. Frozen stiff. That's it, really. I don't know who the bloke was or if they ever found out who nicked the jacket or what.'

Ginny sat there in the dark, her mind spinning. She could see it: the white desolation, the car abandoned on the bridge, a dark figure making off with the warm fur-lined jacket . . .

'It is true?' she managed to say.

'True? Well, as far as I know. It happened a long time back, mind. Ten, fifteen years, maybe more. Why d'you want to know?'

'I don't know. I just went up there the other day, and I heard it was called the broken bridge. I just wondered . . .'

They were trying to start the generator outside. Ginny was glad of the noise, because it helped to cover up the shaking of her voice, and glad of the dark, because there were tears in her eyes. Suddenly the generator caught, and the power came on again.

A siren howled beside them, the carriage lurched forward, one final skeleton sat up in its coffin, and then they were outside, blinking and shielding their eyes from the bright day.

'Sorry about that,' said the boy in charge, hauling the carriages forward.

Andy was trying to get him to refund the fares.

'They could be severely psychologically damaged,' he said, rubbing his hands together. 'Exposing them to spiritual dangers and phantom anxieties, it's a case for the law courts.'

The boy looked down at him. 'Piss off,' he sneered.

'Ah, yes,' said Andy. 'I see your point. Very well argued case. Sounds watertight to me . . .'

They left the Ghost Train and wandered out of the fair. It was nearly time to go home. Ginny wondered what Dad was doing now, whether he'd seen Robert yet, when the funeral would be, a dozen other questions; but more than that, she found herself gripped by the story of the broken bridge. Deep inside her, something had been changed, and she knew that the story was part of her now, part of what made her what she was. But as for what it meant . . .

'It was nice in there,' said Dafydd, getting into the car. 'I liked it.'

'What?' said Andy.

'The Ghost Train. You could have a nice nap in there if it wasn't haunted, like. Ah, well. Let's go home, see if Gertie's got into my sleeping bag.'

Someone had been murdered in the woods. Ginny knew what 'murdered' meant, because Maeve had told her: it meant someone cutting you with a knife so that all your blood ran out, and in a few seconds you were dead. When Ginny looked out of the caravan window she saw dark water dripping off the leaves, running down each surface, and pouring off the point like a little spout. And there was water inside the caravan too, because the window was misty with tiny little drops of it. When you drew on it with your finger, you squashed them together and made a little river, and it ran in a jerk to the bottom.

The gaslight made a hissing noise. Maeve told her that another little girl had touched it and her skin had stuck to the bright part and come right away, so she had one finger that was only bones, no skin, no fingernail, just like a skeleton.

One day it stopped raining, and Ginny and Dawn played outside with two sheets of hard-board. They stood on one and put the other one down on the wet grass ahead of them, and then stepped on to that and put the first one down in front, and so on. They mustn't touch the wet grass or they'd be poisoned and die, but there at the side of the field the grass was long and bent over the boards, so they were both poisoned and dead many times. Then they reached the tree at the edge of the woods where the person had been cut with the knife, and Ginny whispered all about it in Dawn's ear. Her hair smelled funny. Dawn began to cry. She told Maeve when they went in for their dinner, and Maeve hit Ginny, crack, on the leg. Ginny was so surprised she could hardly breathe.

Another time she climbed onto Maeve's bunk when Maeve wasn't there, and found a little door. Ginny thought it would open on to the roof, but when she unclicked it she found a little cupboard there, hanging above the bunk like a tiny room. There was a bottle and a glass, and some cigarettes, and Maeve's make-up, and two books. She and Dawn put on some lipstick and pretended to smoke. They didn't light the cigarettes, but Maeve found out anyway and smacked them both. Cigarettes had a nice smell, but they made Dawn cough, so she had to breathe very carefully. Ginny lay in her top bunk and held her breath for Dawn as long *as she could, listening to the thin beat of Maeve's cassette recorder through the folding partition, and the hissing of the gaslight, and the steady drip of rain from the dark leaves bleeding on to the roof.*

Chapter Seven
The white cuckoo

Dad came home at half past ten that night. Ginny was waiting for him, and as soon as she heard the car turn into the lane she went to the fridge, intending to get out a can of lager for him; but there were none left. When he came in, looking exhausted, he dropped the car keys on the table, kissed her, and kicked off his shoes. She felt tender and protective. What could she do to look after him?

'Make us both a cup of cocoa,' he said. 'I'm worn out.'

She took it through to the living room, where he was sprawled in his armchair, eyes closed. There was a Mozart piano sonata playing on the stereo.

'Here you are, Dad,' she said. 'Don't go to sleep.'

He sat up and took the mug from her. She sat on the sofa with hers. The windows were open because of the heat, and behind the music she could hear the wide silence of the night, different from the narrow silence of the house. The floor lamp lit the side of his head, throwing his eyes into shadow and emphasizing the line from his nose to the corner of his mouth, so that he looked older and almost haggard. He sipped his cocoa, a child's drink, an old person's drink, and she wondered what it would be like when he was an old man and whether he'd have someone to look after him if she wasn't there. She loved him a lot, she thought.

'How was it?' she said.

'Grim. Difficult. The hospital, the undertaker business, that was straightforward enough. Seeing the boy . . . I hadn't realized what a mess everything was in . . .'

Not knowing what he meant, Ginny couldn't say very much. And just now, seeing him as tired as he was, needing her help, she couldn't ask all the questions she was aching to ask. The mess he'd referred to: who'd left things in a mess? The boy's mother? And surely she must have a family – someone to organize funerals and things without Dad having to do it? No; she couldn't ask. She sat there keeping him company, finishing her cocoa, looking after him, reinforcing him. He was all she had.

But she didn't sleep. Next morning being Sunday, she wasn't needed at the Dragon, so she lay in bed till late, half dozing, half thinking back to when she was very young, trying to remember, trying to catch the little scraps of life before they vanished back into the darkness.

There was a caravan; she was certain of that. They must have had a holiday in a caravan, she and Dad, but it can't have been much of a holiday, because all she remembered was rain, an incessant drumming on the roof, moisture everywhere, damp sheets . . . and some delicious shiver of fear, she had no idea why: secrets, and murder, and horror. But it wasn't real. It was safe, it was a story, she could enjoy it.

Her grandparents – Dad's mother and father – she couldn't enjoy them. No murder there, but the atmosphere of their house, that strange time she spent with them . . . How she'd watched through the glass panel of the kitchen door as Grandma hit Grandad, and seen him turn away in pain, begging her to be quiet, and how she, Ginny, had felt sick and faint with unhappiness.

How strange, though, that they'd never been in touch again. Perhaps Rhiannon was right and they'd quarrelled with Dad; perhaps that was what families did. But they were the only relatives she had. No cousins, no aunts or uncles, and her mother's side of the family were as good as mythical: a wealthy family in Port-au-Prince. She and Dad hadn't needed anyone else, though. They were self-contained. They shared jokes and housework and holidays, and he told her about his work and she told him about her drawing, and even though he'd shared his bed with the breakfast ladies, she knew that they were temporary and she was permanent . . . No, the two of them were self-contained, a perfect relationship, father and daughter: nothing could be better.

And now she had to share it with a brother.

And there were only a few days left before all that world of sharing, all that grown-up friendliness and intimacy, vanished for ever.

How could he? How could he not tell her all these years – let her think she was the only one? How could he do it?

Stupidly, she began to cry. Hating herself for the selfishness that paid no heed to this lost brother, Robert, this bereaved boy coming among strangers, she sobbed into her pillow like a child.

Dad was out when she got up. Avoiding me, she thought. She had some cornflakes, looked in the Arts section of the Sunday paper to see if there were any interesting exhibitions coming up (not that she could get to them, but reading about them was something), and then went down to the harbour.

It was another still, sunny day, the best summer for years, perhaps for ever. It might have been a blessing, Ginny thought; on the other hand, it might have been the greenhouse effect. It might mean that everyone was going to die. In the short time they probably had left, however, it was good to wander along by the estuary looking at the old wreck whose ribs stuck out of the mud at low tide and at the trim little yachts at anchor, to wave at the old porter in the station feeding the cat, to hear Angie singing from the kitchen of the Yacht Club and wave at her through the open door; and to go on down to the edge of the water and, just out of curiosity, take the path that led to the house on stilts by the little railway bridge, where Stuart was staying.

He'd said to come and see him, so she felt no inhibitions about climbing the ladder onto the veranda that ran all the way round the house, and knocking at the door, despite the fact that the port-hole windows were still curtained.

After a minute or so the door opened, and Stuart stood there, wearing black boxer shorts and nothing else, fit and lean and silky-skinned, dazzling, glam-orous, and sleepy. She handed him the Sunday paper the delivery boy had left at the top of the ladder.

'Ginny!' he said. 'What's the time?'

'It's coffee time,' she said. 'Sorry if I woke you.'

'It's all right,' he said. 'Come in.'

The door opened directly into the living room. The atmosphere was close and warm and smelled of something she could only think of as maleness. But there was nothing here to threaten her or make her shy; even nearly naked, Stuart didn't do that. He was beyond being sexy, in Rhiannon's terms, probably because he was so impossibly grown up and handsome, and yet at the same time he wasn't kind, either, if kind meant safe and dull. Ginny felt teased and challenged by something not quite human, something between a frank, innocent animal and a powerful, mocking god.

'Open the curtains,' he said. 'If it's coffee time, I'd better make some. It'll taste better than Andy's.'

The room was shipshape, just like the cabin of a yacht. The portholes were edged with brass, and a ship's clock and a barometer hung side by side on the white-painted wooden wall, and altogether they might have been at sea.

'Can I go on the roof?' she said.

'Help yourself.'

There was a wooden ladder up from the veranda, and the roof itself was decked with planking. Ginny stood at the railing and looked out across the estuary and the Yacht Club from this unfamiliar viewpoint. *I've always wanted to see this house*, she thought, *and now here I am. I must be lucky. I can make things happen by wanting them . . .*

She smelled coffee and climbed down the ladder.

'I love this place,' she said. 'I'll buy it when I'm grown up. And live here.'

'What'll you do for a living?'

They were sitting on the edge of the veranda, the planks already warm under their thighs, the oily water nosing about below them among the reeds, around the little red dinghy, between the wooden piles.

'I'm going to be a painter.'

'Why?'

'Because I'm good at it. Because when I look at things, I think automatically about how I'd draw them, how I'd paint them. And . . . also my mother was a painter. Was going to be a painter. So I'm carrying on for her.'

'The lady from Haiti? They have a lot of painters there.'

'Yeah,' Ginny said, 'primitives. Peasants. I know about them. But she wasn't like that. I can't be, either. See, once you know about Picasso and stuff, Matisse, all the modern painters, well, you can't pretend to be a peasant who's never seen them . . . You're stuck, really. You can't go back; you've got to go forward. My mother, she was studying art properly, like I'm going to do.'

'European art,' said Stuart.

Ginny was silent for a minute or so. There was a question in what he said, and he didn't need to make it any plainer than that; it was exactly what she'd been trying to describe to Andy, and it was his problem with the black kids in Bristol: looking black, sounding white.

'Stuart,' she said, 'd'you think there's a difference between European art and, like, African art?' But that wasn't what she wanted to ask. Before he could reply, she went on: 'I mean, I know of course there is. The subject matter's so different. I mean, in European art all the faces are white ones, all the landscapes are places in England or France or Germany or somewhere, but it's not just what the painting's *about* . . .'

'I remember seeing a painting once,' said Stuart, 'a picture by a Chinese artist who came to England. It's a landscape in the Lake District. And it doesn't look like England at all, it looks completely Chinese, with the mountains sticking up out of the mist, just like they do in classical Chinese paintings.'

'Ah, right,' she said. 'But that's different again. He was seeing it in a Chinese way, that's all. He had a tradition that he belonged to.'

'And you haven't.'

'That's right! It's not as simple as making pictures of black people in a sort of fine-art way. Anybody could do that. A white painter could. I need to find a way that's different . . .'

'African?'

'I'm not African, either. I've seen African sculptures, you know, ritual masks, that kind of thing. They're really strong, really powerful, but I can't . . . relate to them. I don't know what they mean. All that ancestor stuff . . . I mean, I've got English ancestors too, haven't I? It's no good saying like my ancestors were African, so I've got to go back to my *roots*. . . . It was my English ancestors who sold my African ancestors into slavery. Where does that leave me? Am I innocent or guilty or what?'

'You can't go back,' Stuart said. 'You can only go forward. You can't forget, either. You have to use everything you know.'

'That's right! That's just what I mean. I can't pretend to be a Haitian primitive.'

'You've never been to Haiti?'

'No. What's it like?'

'It's in a bad way at the moment. It's been in a bad way for years. Poverty and corruption and violence . . . It's pitiful.'

Ginny said nothing. Words like 'poverty' and 'corruption' sounded like white people condemning black people for being uncivilized and savage, and she was uncomfortable about that. On the other hand, he'd been there, he'd seen it.

'What's voodoo like?' she said.

'It's a real religion. It's not just drums and zombies. There's a whole family of gods, and they come to life. I've seen them.'

'They come to life?'

'They take possession of the worshippers. They enter your head, and you behave like them, speak like them, walk like them. You can recognize them at once.'

He told Ginny about the gods and goddesses, the *loa*: about Agwé, the lord of the sea, and Ogoun, the fiery war god and politician, and Damballah, the serpent god. He told her about Erzulie, the goddess of love, who loved luxury and music and perfume and who wore three wedding rings, one for Agwé, one for Damballah, one for Ogoun; Erzulie, who gave and received love, and whose visitations ended in tragic boundless weeping for the shortness of life, the faithlessness of men.

But the *loa* who caught Ginny's attention most was Ghede, the god of the underworld. He was a joker, a trickster, and as she listened, Ginny imagined him with the face of Andy. Stuart told her that once in the 1920s Ghede had taken possession of dozens and dozens of men at once, and they'd all marched to the National Palace dressed in top hats, tail coats, and dark glasses, demanding money. The president had had no choice but to give it to them: what was a president beside the god of the underworld, especially when he appeared in dozens of copies at once? That's a story for Andy, she thought delightedly. But there was another side to Ghede the joker. He was also known as Baron Samedi, the lord of death, of skulls and bones and tombs; he haunted cemeteries and crossroads; it was through Baron Samedi that zombies were brought up from the grave . . .

Ginny listened, transfixed. Africa was too far back, but Haiti came closer as he spoke; the gods began to stir into life. Seeing how interested she was, Stuart drew some elaborate curly designs, including a heart surrounded by lacy swirls and spiky ornamentation.

'These are *vevers*,' he said. 'The priest draws them in flour on the ground before the *loa* come. This is Erzulie's . . . Sometimes it has a sword through it, like this.'

He drew another version. Ginny was enchanted by the prettiness of them, their mysterious delicacy.

'Thanks a lot,' she said. 'I'm going to go there one

...t of my family. I'm good at French
...ut my best subject apart from art.
...about Creole, though.'

...think you'll manage. I'd like to see your
...sometime. Bring them over.'

...ght! Okay . . .'

I'll have to bring my brother too, she thought. *Can't leave him out. Nothing'll be the same from now on.*

'What was your mother's name?' Stuart asked.

'Anielle. Her family name was Baptiste. Why?'

'Just in case I see any of her paintings.'

'Well, she was only a student, more or less . . .'

'Have you got anything of hers? Any drawings or anything?'

'No . . . No. Nothing. There's nothing left. I don't know why, actually. Dad might have kept something and not told me about it . . . I don't know.'

'There must be something still about. Things don't just vanish; they stand around for years, and then people find them in the attic and sell them for a million pounds. There'll be some of her work around somewhere, I guarantee.'

Ginny looked up at him in surprise. He was right, and she'd never thought about it.

'Yeah,' she said rather breathlessly. 'Right! There must be. *She* wouldn't have thrown it away, and he wouldn't . . .'

'We'll keep our eyes open,' he said.

She finished her coffee and left him to his Sunday paper.

Ginny and Dad agreed that since lamb was likely to make you radioactive, and beef to give you mad cow disease, pork was the only safe meat to have for Sunday lunch – until creeping pig fever was discovered anyway. So it was pork she found Dad taking out of the oven when she got home.

'Hungry?' he said.

'Yeah. Sort of.'

'Who's the man in the boat house?' he said as they sat down.

'He's called Stuart. Did you see me there, then?' She was surprised, as if he'd been spying on her.

'I was looking at someone's boat.'

'Stuart's a friend of Andy's,' she explained.

'Oh, that's all right, then.'

'Why were you looking at a boat?'

'I thought we might get one. Just a dinghy to start with. To learn to sail, so that we can all, I don't know, start something together. Instead of Robert having to fit into a lot of things that grew up without him.'

She was silent, smothering a piece of meat with apple sauce. It was probably a good idea.

'Dad,' she said, 'when Maman died, were there any paintings of hers left? Or drawings, or anything?'

'No,' he said. 'Very little, unfortunately. I suppose it went back to her family.'

'What d'you mean, you suppose? Didn't you have all her things in the house with you? Didn't she leave them to you in her will or something? Or to me?'

He said nothing, finishing his mouthful, going to the fridge, opening a new six-pack of lager, fetching a glass, pouring it, sitting down again; and something in his manner made her put down her knife and fork and watch him, apprehensive.

'Ginny,' he said, 'I was going to put this off for a while, till you were older, but there's no point any more. It's too late, what with Robert coming . . . The thing is . . .'

He took a deep breath. Ginny could see a pulse beating in his temple. He went on:

'Part of the reason I didn't tell you about Janet and Robert was that I'd have to tell you something else as well, the thing I was going to keep. Something about Maman. I should have told you years ago, but I never thought this other business would come up . . . The thing is that we were never married, me and Maman. I was married to Janet. That's why I couldn't . . . Anyway. I was married to

111

Janet, and there was the child, Robert, and then I met Maman, Anielle. The one I should have married. Janet and I . . . well, it wasn't working, it never worked. I was stupid, I was young. And then you were born. And then there was no Maman. So obviously I was . . . I had to look after you. There was no one else. I didn't want anyone else to do it, I wanted you. And here we are, the two of us. If . . . Eventually . . . If she hadn't fallen ill, then one day I'd have told you. I'm so sorry it was forced on us. There's hardly time to take it in before he comes. Can you understand? So to answer your question about paintings and stuff . . . if there were any left, they were packed up and sent back to Haiti, back to her family. There was very little I had, except that photograph. Ginny, I'm sorry.'

There was no end to these surprises, she thought numbly. First I have a long-lost brother, and then he turns out to be the legal son. No – what was the word? Legitimate. So that made her illegitimate. Born out of wedlock. A bastard. That's what they'd have said in the old days.

Not that anyone cared about that now, except that because of it she felt herself being pushed further and further to the edge of things. All the sympathy she'd been carefully educating herself to feel for Robert was blown away in a moment, so it couldn't have been very real, she told herself. She was being shoved aside by this invisible cuckoo, this white son and heir of a proper marriage, while she was the result of something like an affair with a breakfast lady . . .

The food was getting cold on her plate. He wasn't touching his, either.

'When's he coming, this Robert?' she said. Her voice sounded shaky.

'The funeral's on Wednesday. I'll go up for that and bring him back. Ginny, he's a nice boy. None of it's his fault—'

'Oh, sure,' she said savagely. 'It's probably nobody's *fault*. It's probably just something you get, like measles or something. Nobody could have guessed, could they? Absolutely unpredictable . . .'

She'd never felt so angry, never been so surprised at herself, at him, at everything. She shoved her plate away and stood up.

'You don't understand—'

'How can I understand when you don't bloody well tell me things?' she stormed at him, feeling lightning in her eyes.

'Ginny, wait—'

'What's the point? What else are you going to tell me? You found me in a ditch or something?'

'Listen . . . I know I should have told you before;

I've already said I'm sorry about that. I realize now—'

'It's a bit late for that, isn't it? What else is there? What else is he going to do me out of?'

'He's not going to do you out of anything, Ginny, for God's sake—'

'He already has!'

'No, he hasn't. Come on, this doesn't change anything as far as we're concerned. We're the family, you and me; we'll always be OK. He's the one who's lost, he's the one who's hurt.'

'OK! OK! D'you think I don't realize that? I just don't know what else you're keeping from me – I mean, what else *is* there? All that stuff about Haiti – is that not true, either? Did she come from Jamaica or something? Or was she real in the first place? Did you just get me from a children's home? Or maybe she wasn't an artist – is that it? Maybe she was just a shop assistant or something, maybe you just fancied her when you went in to buy a pair of socks, and then you were stuck with *me* as a result—'

'Ginny, this isn't getting us anywhere. If you knew how much I wish—'

'I don't care what you wish, Dad, I really don't.'
'At least let me—'

'And you couldn't even keep her paintings! Couldn't even keep *one* of them!'

She flung her chair aside and rushed out, slamming the door, and ran down towards the beach, away from the house, away from home, away from him.

Chapter Eight
Robert

So Ginny still had no answer to the question at the front of her mind: what was he like, this brother? She'd wanted to ask when Dad came home the night before but, feeling sorry for him, hadn't brought it up; she'd been going to ask that morning but he'd gone out; and now they wouldn't speak till one of them made the first move toward friendliness again. They so seldom had rows that this state was uncomfortable, unfamiliar, and Ginny found herself wondering what exactly she had said, and whether any of it was unforgivable.

But it was his fault, she told herself savagely, as she sat in the dunes and trickled hot sand over her bare feet. He had no right to keep that secret. I should have known . . .

Finding out something about yourself that other people have known and haven't told you makes you feel stupid, as if they were laughing at you for being so naive. Dad had known, this Janet had known, even Robert had known – they'd all known Dad wasn't married to Maman; it was only she who hadn't. She felt angry, and foolish, and sorry for herself.

She stayed out till five o'clock, dozing in the dunes, wandering among the rock pools, gazing for half an hour or more at one particular sea anemone; and she went home at half past five only because it was nearly time for the Yacht Club.

The restaurant was never very busy on Sundays, so there might have been time to sit and chat with Andy, except that he was in a surly, scratchy mood for once; or it might have been that the whole world was irritated and ill at ease with itself. On the way home again, she found herself wandering, more and more slowly, wishing time itself would stop.

Dad was watching television with half his attention, the rest being paid to some papers spread out on a board across his lap.

'There's some salad in the kitchen,' he said shortly.

'I had something to eat at the Yacht Club,' she said, pausing inside the door.

The silence between them trembled for a moment. If he'd looked up at her it might have broken, but he didn't.

She pretended to look at the TV for a moment and then went out and shut the door.

Actually, she hadn't eaten at the Yacht Club, and

as she had hardly started her lunch before the row began, she was hungry. Ignoring the salad, she cut some bread and spread it thickly with peanut butter and took it, with her sketch pad and charcoal, up to the main road.

There she sat on the wall in the golden light and tried to capture the precise way the road dipped and curved, flowing like a grey river between its grassy banks. Charcoal was better than pencil for that – you could rub it on thickly, push it around with your fingers, express the flow of it. This was still her kingdom, after all; she hadn't been disinherited of that. And she claimed it not through birth but through love and talent, and she thought sometimes, when she looked at her work as objectively as she could, that she *was* talented. This sketch was alive. It showed not only the road but her feelings about the road; it expressed movement and restlessness and energy.

Working, she decided, was the best thing in the world. Even better than knowing who you were was knowing what you had to do.

As she drifted down to the house again in the dusk, she wondered if her mother had felt like that. Those lost paintings . . . If only she could find them! They might show her the answer to that unspoken question of Stuart's, the problem of how to paint, the problem of finding a tradition for herself.

But she felt strong, as she let herself in, strong and in control. She pinned up the drawing beside her bedroom door and looked at it as she got undressed for bed. It was good. She was going to find a language, even if she had to invent one.

And as she went to sleep, she thought: Suppose the pictures *are* still around somewhere? They might not have wanted them, this Haitian family. They might just be in storage, or even in a gallery. Anything might have happened; Dad might not have told all the truth still.

Wednesday, when it came, was an anticlimax. Dad phoned from Liverpool, after the funeral, to say that he'd be coming home alone after all: Wendy Stevens would be bringing Robert down the next day.

It felt like being reprieved, but it left her frustrated. What could she do with this freedom? She spent most of it, in fact, with Rhiannon, staying overnight at her house and leaving a message on the kitchen table for Dad to see when he got home on Wednesday night.

They'd come to a sort of truce by that time. They'd had to; neither of them wanted anger in the air when Robert arrived. So they'd talked a little more, but Dad still hadn't told her much about Robert. Her brother was quiet, reserved, polite, with dark hair, and that was all she learned. So for Ginny, he was still little more than a blank, which she filled in alternately with a cold, evil, triumphant usurper and with a bewildered, lost, unhappy semi-orphan. The latter idea was largely Rhiannon's, and Rhiannon had a different idea about Ginny's own background too. It was much better like this, she said; it was really romantic to have your parents unmarried; it showed she was a child of passion, Robert merely one of duty. Ginny wasn't convinced.

Thursday passed in a jumpy, nervous blur. Wendy Stevens and Robert were due at half past five, and Dad said he'd be back from work in time to greet them. Ginny had got the evening off from the Yacht Club, and she spent the afternoon with Rhiannon, getting a lavish tea together: finding the one table-cloth they had, ironing it, setting the tea out on the lawn with currant bread and butter, scones, jam, ginger cake, and the bone-china tea set they'd bought for some reason years before and never used. The tea was her idea: her contribution. She hadn't told Dad.

'We're going to leave decorating his bedroom till he comes,' she said. 'Let him choose. I suppose that's best, really.'

'Suppose you fall in love with him?' Rhiannon said. She was lying in the hammock watching Ginny fussing with cups and saucers. 'Apparently it often happens.'

'What d'you mean?'

'When long-lost brothers and sisters meet. They fall in love,' Rhiannon said complacently. 'With what they've got in common, it's just too much to control. There's an irresistible sexual current . . .'

'Oh, don't be stupid. I never heard anything so bloody cracked, even from you.'

'Well, don't say I didn't warn you. God, I'd better go. They'll be here soon.'

She scrambled up, but Ginny shoved her back. 'No! Listen! I just remembered something. You know the broken bridge? Pont Doredig?'

'Yeah? What of it?'

'Dafydd Lewis told me the story. Did you know what happened?'

Rhiannon shook her head. 'Something about a car crash . . . I don't know. What was it, then?'

Ginny told her what Dafydd had said. As she recounted the story of the abandoned baby in its fur-lined coat, and the coat's disappearance and the baby's death, she found her eyes pricking embarrassingly with tears. Luckily, Rhiannon was just as affected. But Ginny had something else to add.

'Listen,' she said. 'I saw Joe Chicago at the fair. Close up. And I saw his jacket, and *that* had a fur lining . . .'

'Oh, don't be stupid! It couldn't be him.'

'It *could* be.'

'Oh, go on. That's mad . . .'

'But listen . . . He was in jail, wasn't he?'

'Yeah, but—'

'And it was about fifteen years ago, Dafydd reckons, and Joe Chicago must be thirty at least, so he could have been fifteen or more then . . . He could easily have done it.'

Rhiannon watched her, pretending a sceptical look.

'The thing is . . .'

'What? I bet I'm right. I bet that's what he went to jail for.'

'The thing is I don't reckon that story's necessarily true. I mean . . . who'd go off and leave their child alone in a car like that?'

'Plenty of people,' Ginny said firmly. 'It happens all the time. Anyway, I *know* it's true. I bet if we looked through the paper we'd find it, eventually, in the files in the library . . . Hey, could your sister ask her husband about it?'

Rhiannon's face was too mobile and expressive to hide her interest. She wasn't convinced, but Ginny, seeing she was intrigued, felt a shiver of pleasure: here was something other than Robert to occupy herself with. A private mystery.

'Well, she might,' said Rhiannon.

'Let's go and ask her!'

'What, now?'

'No; course not. Later on sometime. I'd like to see her again anyway.'

'Okay,' said Rhiannon, nodding. Then she rolled over and got out of the hammock. 'I'm going to go. I'm getting nervous – they'll be here in a minute.'

'Don't tell her about it before we go,' Ginny said. 'I want to ask her myself.'

'All right. But I bet you're wrong.'

'I'm right,' said Ginny. 'No question.'

At half past five, Ginny heard Dad's car turn into the lane. She shut the comic she'd been reading and swung one leg over the side of the hammock. She'd been afraid Wendy Stevens would arrive first, leaving Ginny to meet Robert on her own.

She looked down at the tablecloth spread out, the milk jug, the sugar bowl, the teaspoons, and suddenly thought how pretentious, how fake, what a condescending gesture it was. Was it too late to put it all away? Hide it, pretend it had never crossed her mind?

She heard Dad opening the front door and then heard another car turning into the lane and stopping, and Dad calling to someone, 'Hi! You made it, then,' in a false, hearty voice; and she lay back, thinking: *Well, it's not such a big thing. He might be really nice, and I don't have to spend all the time with him anyway. Brothers and sisters don't necessarily, do they?*

'Where's Ginny? Ah! Lazing in the hammock!' Cringe-making jolliness, she thought. *Please* be natural, Dad . . .

She sat up. Wendy Stevens was just coming out of the kitchen door, dressed in a suit again, looking too hot, too strained.

'Hi,' she said, and Ginny smiled and stood up.

Behind her was Dad, and behind him was Robert.

They looked at each other with instant, savage, and mutual hatred.

She saw a thin, stoop-shouldered boy with pale skin and lank brown hair. His face was narrow, foxy, and sullen. Everything about him, every line of his body – and she prided herself on reading appearances – spoke of suspicion, reserve, a sort of mistrustful contempt. He was taller than she was by a couple of inches, and she found herself standing up straight and holding her chin high to face him. There was a moment's silence while they measured each other like that, and then Wendy said, 'Hey! What's all this? Been making tea for us, then?'

'Ginny, why don't you show Robert the bathroom?' said Dad.

He was nervous. He hadn't said a thing about all the work she'd put into getting this bloody tea ready. She just nodded.

'It's this way,' she said to Robert, coldly, and went past him into the kitchen.

She saw a shabby suitcase in the hall, standing next to a dusty cardboard box containing cassettes. Was that all he had to bring with him? Now she was confused again, as if she felt pity.

'I'm sorry about your mum,' she said, not looking at him.

He said nothing. She thought he was just being rude, until she caught a glimpse of his expression: it was one of utter misery.

'Your bedroom's here,' she said, opening the door on the landing, 'and the bathroom's over there. There's a loo downstairs as well.'

He nodded. He hadn't spoken yet.

On her way back, she glanced into the box of cassettes and saw names she'd never heard of. No clue there, then.

'Ginny, this is a smashing tea,' said Wendy Stevens, buttering a scone.

'Yeah, well, I thought . . .'

'Great, love,' said Dad.

Dad was sitting on the grass, Wendy in the deck-chair. She exchanged a look with Ginny; Dad wasn't looking at either of them.

'Your dad tells me you've got an evening job,' she said. 'Are you working tonight?'

'No. I've got the time off. It's not much anyway. I'm just helping in the kitchen of this restaurant.'

'Because I thought we might have a chat, maybe, before I go.'

'Oh, right. OK. Are you going back to Liverpool tonight?'

'I've got to. Busy morning tomorrow. Ah, Robert, love . . .'

He came and sat awkwardly on the grass, as far away from Ginny as he could get while still being approximately part of the group.

'Tuck in,' said Dad. 'Ginny's done a good job here.'

Oh, these scalp-crawling pleasantries, how they made Ginny cringe, and how she wished she'd just spent the afternoon hanging about with Andy or Stuart and rolled in later, casual, indifferent. When you try to be friendly you expose yourself to so many embarrassments, she thought. It's probably better to be selfish and say to hell with it, let him sink, we never asked him to come here.

She wasn't aware of how rebellious and angry her expression was becoming, nor of how she was shredding a paper napkin between her fingers, folding and tearing, folding and tearing, her eyes down, staring at nothing.

Wendy Stevens saw, though, and put her plate down. 'Ginny,' she said, 'come and show me where your restaurant is.'

Ginny blinked and nodded. 'Right,' she said, standing up.

Robert watched them go from the corner of his eyes. He still hadn't said a word.

'I don't really want to see the restaurant,' said Wendy as they walked out into the lane. 'Anywhere'll do.'

'We could go down to the beach, if you want.'

'OK. Anywhere.'

As they walked, Ginny trailed her hand along the warm stones of the wall. 'You know what this feels like?' she said after a minute or so.

'What? Tell me.'

'It feels like being invaded. He doesn't belong here. He obviously doesn't want to be here. He obviously hates me.'

'Stop feeling sorry for yourself.'

127

'I'm not; it's a fact. Couldn't you see how he looked at me? I'm not bothered by what he thinks anyway; it makes no difference.'

'No difference to what?'

'To what I feel. I hate him.'

'Well, that's honest.'

'I'd hate him if he was invading this place or not, brother or not, whoever he was. There's people you just instinctively hate, whoever they are, and there's nothing you can do about it.'

She looked at Wendy defiantly, almost as if she was expecting her to do just that, to do something about Ginny's hating him. But Wendy just walked slowly along, her eyes half-closed against the sun.

'What did your dad tell you?' she said.

'Bloody liar he is too,' Ginny said. 'See, I can't trust anyone any more. He told me after all these years, all this time, he told me on Sunday that he wasn't married to my mother after all. He was married to Robert's mum.'

'That's right. They never divorced, you see. Never even legally separated. Did he not tell you that?'

'No.'

'Did he tell you anything about your mother?'

'Nothing new, except that he wasn't married to her. I'm beginning to wonder if she was true anyway, whether he just made her up. He's always told me she was an art student, see . . . And that's very important to me, because I want to be a painter too – that's the most important thing in my life.'

'The most important thing?'

'Yeah. Absolutely the only thing. Because I think I'm like her, see, my mother, I'm kind of doing it for her, doing the things she couldn't do. I'm going to grow up and live and be a painter in the way she couldn't. And if it turns out that . . . This is going to sound really snobbish, really *horrible*, right, but . . . if it turns out that she wasn't an artist at all but a shop assistant or something, then I'm going to feel really *cheated*. Because her being an artist, that's something proud, something to live up to. That's something to inherit. Especially now . . . Especially now he's come. Robert. Now he's the . . . the sort of real one. I've got nothing, except her. So . . . That's why it's important.'

They walked on slowly. Insects were chirping in the grass at the foot of the wall; the sun beat up at them from the bronze-coloured sea beyond the dunes.

'I told him he had to tell you,' said Wendy. 'It wasn't fair. But *he* feels terrible about the whole business. Robert's sixteen; he could have stayed in care for a couple of years, till he finishes at school, but your dad felt it was right to do this—'

'Did anyone ask Robert what he wanted?' Ginny asked.

'Yes. I did. Naturally. He wasn't in a state to make that sort of decision. He was very close to his mum.'

'There aren't any more, are there? No more brothers or sisters hidden away? No, I suppose not. How can I get on with him? What can I do?'

'Just be yourself. You don't have to put on an act.'

'To be myself, I *have* to put on an act,' Ginny said bitterly.

'What's that mean?'

'It means I don't know who I am.'

'I thought you said you were an artist. Just be that.'

They walked on for a minute or two.

'Wendy,' Ginny said, 'suppose someone's adopted, right, and they don't know they are, or they think they are and no one'll tell them . . . Can they find out?'

'That's not the usual question I get,' Wendy said, stopping to lean over a gate. 'The usual one is: I know I'm adopted, and can I find my mother?'

'And can they?'

'When they're eighteen, yes. But as for your problem – why d'you think you're adopted?'

'Well . . . The thing is, after this . . . I mean, now

130

I'm finding out a load of things I never knew, and it's got me thinking. There's things I can't sort out in my mind, things I remember from way way back, and I ask Dad about them and he doesn't know. Or just pretends. Like there was this caravan, I was staying in it, near some woods, and it was raining and raining, and I wasn't with Dad . . . I used to think I remembered him there, but now I know I didn't. There was me and this other little girl, and there was a woman in charge of us. She had red hair and she smoked all the time. And she drank gin. I know that because the other night, in the restaurant, I smelt the smell of gin and it all came back . . . Dad never has gin in the house, he doesn't like it, so I hadn't smelt it for a long time. But it brought it all back. And that's not the only thing . . .'

She told Wendy about the time she'd stayed with her grandparents, that unhappy, inexplicable few days in the middle of nothing.

'So where was Dad? There's a whole stack of memories without him, and they're all kind of scattered, and then he starts coming into them and they're all joined up and I know where I am, then: it's kind of connected to me. But all those early ones he's not in.'

She looked carefully at Wendy and saw she was listening. Ginny went on:

131

'Because I heard something about Dad the other day that I could never ask him. Someone said they'd heard he'd been in prison, only they didn't know what for. And . . .'

She shrugged.

Wendy said, 'If that's true, then it would explain why you can't remember him early on. But that doesn't mean you're adopted as well. You ought to ask him.'

'I can't. But say I *was* adopted: how could I find out for certain?'

Wendy looked doubtful. 'There's the adoption register: you could write and ask if your name's on that. Or you could write and ask for your birth certificate. But they both take time and cost money. And if you'd been born abroad, there might not be a birth certificate in your name anyway, or your real name might be different . . . I'm not sure what you'd learn from the adoption register, either; I've never had to answer this question before.'

'Can you tell me the address?'

'Not now; I don't know it offhand. I'll send it to you. What was your mother's name?'

'Baptiste. Anielle Baptiste.'

'You might be registered under her name, that's all.'

'You mean Howard might not be my name?'

'It depends how it was registered. D'you remember anything else about this caravan?'

Ginny closed her eyes, trying to catch the flickering memories as they darted through her mind like little fish in a rockpool.

'The woman was Catholic. There was a crucifix on the wall, I remember that. She was called . . . Maeve? I don't know how you'd spell it. And the other little girl was called Dawn. Oh, yeah, and someone had been murdered in the woods.'

She opened her eyes to see Wendy looking at her sharply.

'I just remember someone telling me,' Ginny explained. 'These woods by the caravan, all dripping wet and cold, someone had been killed there. We were dead scared . . . I think. I *think* that was it. That's all I remember.'

'You must have been very young.'

'Well, that's the point: too young to remember. Anyway.' She shrugged.

'I'd better be getting back,' Wendy said. 'I'll send you that address.'

'Can I ask you something? Something personal?'

Wendy looked surprised, but nodded.

'Why do you wear a suit?' Ginny asked. 'It must be ever so hot. And you'd look much nicer without it. More natural.'

'If you don't wear a suit these days, people think you're not working hard,' Wendy said. 'They want value for money.'

'I'm never going to wear a suit.'

'You get used to it. You get used to anything. Even having a brother.'

Ginny made a face. 'Yeah, well,' she said.

They walked slowly back to the house.

One day Ginny and Dad got in the car and just drove away for miles and miles, and then Dad drove the car on to a ship and when he drove it off they were in another country, where even the chocolate tasted different.

And they drove on and on until it was nearly night, and there was no house to sleep in, no bed to lie on, no food to eat. Ginny thought they'd have to sleep in the wilds.

Then Dad stopped and opened the back of the car and took out a tent, and there were big soft bags to sleep in, and a little stove that he cooked some sausages and beans on. Everything they needed, and it was all so neat! She'd never dreamed anyone could be so clever.

That was their first holiday, and every year they went off like that, heading for anywhere else. They'd drive off the ferry, and he'd say, 'Left or right?' and she'd choose, on the spur of the moment, and whenever they came to a crossroads she'd decide which way to go. They never knew where *they'd end up. One year they went as far north as they could get, along the coast of Norway and into the Arctic Circle, where the sun never set. They sat out in the open at midnight, playing cards, eating strange meals: fried fish and chocolate sauce, cherry pie and chutney, as if it were the most natural thing in the world.*

They went everywhere. One day in Milan he took her to a fashionable shop and bought her the most beautiful dress in the world, and that evening they went to the opera. In his dinner jacket and his black bow tie he looked like a king, and she felt like not his daughter but his queen; and the audience clapped and cheered, not for the singers or the orchestra but for Ginny's dress, and for her handsome father, and for the elegant, mysterious way they looked together, stars, a king and a queen, beyond the reach of envy or despair.

Chapter Nine
The barbecue

During the next couple of days Ginny and Robert spoke about five times. Their longest conversation took place on Friday, late in the afternoon. Dad had taken some time off to be at home for a while, and after lunch he and Robert had gone down to the harbour to look at boats; and now he'd gone into town for some shopping, leaving Ginny and Robert alone together for the first time.

Robert was in the hammock, and Ginny, seeing him from the kitchen, didn't know whether to ignore him and go to her room or make the effort and talk. She didn't want to stay indoors, she wanted to go into the garden; and whether it was that or the feeling that she ought to be nice to Robert, in the end she went out, sat in the shade of the tree, and said, 'Hi.'

He'd been pretending to be asleep. He opened his eyes, frowning.

'Hello,' he said.

'Did you see any good boats?'

'Dunno. I dunno anything about boats.'

'Dad thought maybe we could all learn to sail.'

He sniffed.

'Robert . . . Did you know about Dad and me before this happened?'

'I knew about him. Obviously. She might have mentioned you, I don't know.'

'What did she tell you about him?'

'She told me who he was, that's all.'

'Did she say why they weren't living together?'

'I never asked.'

He seemed to be on the verge of adding something, and she waited, but nothing came. She thought that if she told him that Dad had never mentioned him, it might sound as if he didn't care. It was so difficult to find anything to say.

Finally she said, 'Did you ever visit his parents? Grandad and Grandma?'

'We didn't have anything to do with them.'

'What, nothing? Why?'

'Because my mum – my mother didn't get on with them. I dunno. She never said.'

His voice was cold with scorn, and it kept breaking; she could tell he was self-conscious about it. She tried again.

'Did you actually live in Liverpool?'

No. Outside.'

'I've only been there a couple of times . . .'

Silence.

'Did your mum have any other relations?' she said.

He swung himself out of the hammock and faced her furiously.

'Can't you bloody well shut up about her? Leave her alone! Just bloody shut up!'

His pale face was blotched with anger. He was quivering all over. Before she could even think what to say, before she could even feel shocked, he was gone, slamming the kitchen door after him.

She looked down at her fingers, twined in her lap. Maybe she had asked too many questions about his mother, but there wasn't much else to talk about. *Narrow self-righteous prim stuck-up superior constipated pig*, she thought. OK, *if he doesn't want to talk, that's fine; suits me.*

She'd been going to offer to make them some coffee. Instead she left the house and set off for the Yacht Club early, calling in at the caravan first to say hello to Dafydd. She found him sprawled on the step, reading *Love and Rockets*.

'Is that the new one?' she said. 'Has Hopey come back yet?'

'No, she's having a bad time, Hopey is. Get off! You can have it when I've finished. How's your brother, then?'

She'd told him and Andy about it all, hesitantly at first, but finding them as fascinated as Rhiannon. She'd thought boys weren't as interested in relationships as girls were; this would teach her to be sexist, she'd thought.

'I've just had a row with him,' she said, and told him about it. 'I don't know what I did wrong. I can't just say nothing about his mother, can I? And there's not much else I can ask him about.'

'Well, he's probably feeling bad,' Dafydd said. 'Bound to be. Just leave him alone for a bit; he'll be all right.'

Looking at Dafydd's strong oil-stained hands, his big slow kind face, she felt like kissing him. Why hadn't he a girlfriend? There was a story that he'd gone out with Carol Barnes once upon a time and didn't kiss her till the fourth date, and then only because she made him. Ginny couldn't remember who'd told her that. It was probably Rhiannon, and she'd probably made it up.

'You ought to fetch him down here,' Dafydd said. 'He can go a couple of rounds with Gertie.'

'Isn't she finished yet?'

'I'm going to take her out and bury her tonight, I tell you. But then she'd probably dig herself out and lie there howling. Hey, if we hid her in old man Alston's house, they might think it was haunted.'

140

'Dafydd . . . You know what you told me about Pont Doredig?'

'Aye.'

'Well, I've been thinking. . . . It might have been Joe Chicago who did it. Who took the jacket. Because *his* jacket's fur-lined; I saw it at the pinball table.'

'Yeah, but . . . *Duw*, there's lots of jackets like that. Anyway, it's just a story. It's probably not true. He wouldn't still have it, would he? The police would have got it off him and given it back to the bloke in the car.'

'He might have hidden it,' she said. 'I bet I'm right. And it *is* true, I know it.'

She could see it in her mind's eye as clearly as her father's face or her mother's photograph: the snow-covered road, the moonlight, the car, the broken parapet, the dark figure, the jacket, the baby crying on the empty seat. She found herself laying it out like a comic strip: a wide panel here to show the emptiness, the wide white desolation, with the little car at the centre crumpled darkly on the bridge; and a close-up there to show the face of the killer, the thief, Joe Chicago's face, blurred as if through the misted glass of the car window . . . It would be almost entirely in black and white, but with subtle greys and browns and ghost-coloured shadows.

She could do that. She could paint it. A painting laid out like a comic strip; or a tragic strip.

The idea gave her a little thrill of pleasure. She realized that Dafydd was saying something and came back to the present.

'What?' she said.

'I says take no notice of your brother; leave him. He'll be all right. I remember when Gwilym's mam died, he hardly spoke for a year.'

He went back to *Love and Rockets*.

'See you, then,' Ginny said, and drifted off towards the Yacht Club.

As she turned into the field that led along beside the estuary, she heard someone call her name, and turned to see Glyn Williams coming toward her. She stopped to wait for him.

Glyn was about her own age. He lived in the village, where his parents kept the greengrocery, and although she hadn't had much to do with him, she liked him well enough. She was probably going to see more of him next year, because like her he was one of the few who'd opted to do French at A Level.

'Hi,' he said. 'I've been looking all over for you. Who's that at your house?'

'Oh, that's Robert. My brother. My half-brother, really.'

'Well, well. I didn't know. Anyway, listen . . . We're going to have a barbecue tomorrow night. Eryl, Siân, all the rest, the usual thing. Bring your brother, why not?'

'Oh, great. Well, I don't know if he'll come, but *I* will. Thanks.'

'See you, then . . .'

He gave a grin and turned away. He was a strange boy, she thought, abrupt and quirky and not bad-looking, with his dark-red curly hair and his lean, muscular body. For some reason she thought of what she'd said to Wendy Stevens, about not wanting to discover that her mother had been a shop assistant, and alone as she was, she blushed; because Glyn's father earned his living in a shop, but he was a bard too, a Welsh poet well known in the *eisteddfodau* where poets and musicians competed for prizes, and he had two published collections to his name. He was at least as much of an artist as Ginny's mother, in fact. Nothing was as simple as it seemed.

When she told Robert the next morning about the barbecue and made it clear he was invited too, he nodded and said, 'Yeah. OK, I don't mind.'

She was so surprised by his mildness that she didn't know what to say next.

That was at breakfast. He and Dad were going into Porthafon – to get Robert some decent clothes, Dad had told her when Robert had gone to the bathroom; he only had what was in that tatty suitcase.

'I don't know what she thought she was doing,' he said. 'Maybe she'd been ill for longer than I thought. Are you getting on with him all right?'

Ginny thought: Why don't you look, and then you'd see? But she said, 'Yeah, fine . . . Dad? You know your parents? Grandad and Grandma? Where did they live? Was that Liverpool too?'

'Not far away. Chester, as a matter of fact.'

'Robert said his mother didn't get on with them.'

'Oh, really?' He was trying to fold back the newspaper and making heavy weather of it, flapping it back and forth to get the crease straight.

'Was his name the same as yours?'

'Whose name?'

'Grandad's, of course.'

'What d'you want to know that for, for goodness' sake?'

'I just want to know about myself,' she said, looking at him openly. 'About my family.'

He didn't look at her. 'His name's Ken. Kenneth

Henry Howard. Her name's Dorothy. Now, is there anything you want in Porthafon?'

'No, thanks,' she said demurely.

The reason she'd given for wanting to know her grandfather's name was true, but not the whole truth. As soon as Dad and Robert had gone, she phoned Directory Enquiries and asked for the number of Mr K. H. Howard of Chester.

The operator found it at once.

'Can you give me his address?' Ginny asked.

'Sixteen Grove Road,' said the operator.

So now she had her grandparents' name and address and telephone number. Feeling pleased with this secret knowledge, she went off to the Dragon and told Rhiannon, who hadn't been there to hear it the day before, everything she knew about Robert.

On Saturday evening, the Yacht Club was busy. Ginny sensed the atmosphere as soon as she walked in.

'Ah, here's my little girlfriend,' Andy said, whisking something creamy in a bowl.

'You haven't got a girlfriend, you pillock,' said Angie Lime wearily. 'Hurry up with that sauce. I need it chop-chop.'

There were six chickens ready instead of the usual four, and Angie was cursing about the vegetables, because the supplier hadn't delivered any courgettes. Ginny, caught up in the busy-ness, swung into the routine at once; this was somewhere she felt at home. She cut the bread, filled the baskets, took them into the restaurant, picked up the salt and pepper shakers for filling. Harry was fiddling with the beer tap.

'How's old Picasso? Has old Calvert sold any pictures yet?'

'Yes, he has, actually,' Ginny told him. 'He sold one today for forty pounds.'

'Get away!' said Harry. 'He never!'

'He did, I was there. There was a young couple having coffee, and the man was really keen on them, but she wasn't, I could tell. Mr Calvert was telling them all about the pictures, what they meant, and finally the man said, "I'll buy one." I could see her expression. He's probably regretting it now.'

Harry chortled, slapping his hands together like a performing seal. 'What sort of picture was it?' he said.

'He does all these sort of science-fantasy ideas . . . This one was called *Alchemical Harmony*. There were three glass jar things floating in space, with a nude woman in one of them.'

'And that was it? A naked woman in a jar, and he gets forty quid for it?'

'And two other jars,' she said, laughing too.

'Fantastic . . . Have you told Angie? *Duw*, that's a good one. Have an olive, go on.'

He threw one in the air, tried to catch it in his mouth, missed, and laughed again. She took one for herself and went back to the kitchen, where she found Andy on his own.

'Harry reckons we'll do the ton tonight,' he told her.

'What's that mean?'

'Do a hundred dinners. We had ninety-two last Saturday. That's why Angie's in a panic.'

'Are you coming to the barbecue?'

'Oh, yeah, I'll be along later. Is your brother coming?'

'Yeah. I think so.'

'What's it like, having a white brother?'

He couldn't have asked that with Angie Lime there, and she knew it.

'He doesn't seem like anything to do with me,' she said. 'We've got nothing in common at all . . .'

He looked up from the onions he was chopping. His eyes were bright, his face shiny with heat and brimful of vivid life and mockery. She felt her heart beat faster, felt as if the world was full of possibilities, that anything might happen; but Angie Lime came back into the kitchen, and the moment passed.

The first customers were arriving. It was time to work.

When she went home she had a shower and washed and oiled her hair, and then spent a long time deciding what to wear. It was only the beach, but it wasn't only the beach, because Andy would be there, and she wanted to look as good as she would if she felt good, which, she found rather surprisingly, she did. No jeans tonight, no cycling shorts, nothing clinging and Lycra tight. She wanted to look Haitian, or at least Caribbean. A wide flowered skirt, a white top that left her arms bare, a pink silk scarf twisting into a roll and tied around her hair; and then, hesitantly, a drop of perfume on her throat – sandalwood, which she liked for its heavy tropical richness.

So she was ready, and she went to the living room to find Robert.

His eyes widened in brief surprise when he saw her, and she was surprised too, because he'd combed his hair back and shaved, or washed, or something; and he was wearing a new cream-coloured shirt and black jeans, and altogether, she thought, Rhiannon would approve.

'OK, then?'

He got up. Dad was watching, half anxious, half relieved that they seemed to be getting on.

'Back by midnight,' he said.

'Oh, go on, Dad! We'll have hardly any time there!' she said.

'All right. Just this once. When do *you* suggest?'

'One o'clock? Since it's summer?'

'One o'clock. If you're not back then, I'll come down there with a torch.'

'Thanks. And can I take some lager?'

'You're supposed to be making money. Buy your own.'

'Not allowed to. *Please . . .*'

'Two cans, then. And pay me back.'

She kissed him, and they left. Both she and Dad knew that this was a performance for Robert: wheedling sister, indulgent father. What Robert made of it she couldn't tell, because he was looking sullen again, and he obviously wasn't going to speak unless she spoke first.

God, I wish I'd asked Rhiannon to come to the house first, she thought.

'I got some bratwurst,' she said in desperation after a couple of minutes. 'You know, German sausages. For the barbecue. I saw them in the deli in town this morning. Dad and me, when we went to Germany last year on holiday, we had them all the time.'

'I haven't brought anything,' he said.

'It's all right; this is for both of us. We usually have a couple of barbecues like this every summer. Last year it was raining too much. But it's not special or anything; it's just some kids from the village, that's all. I'm sorry if I went on about your mum yesterday. It was different when my mum died, 'cause I never knew her, obviously.'

'She dead, then?'

'Didn't Dad say? She died when I was born. But I won't ask about your mum any more. I was just interested. You know . . .'

He sniffed. 'Yeah,' he said.

The walk down toward the sunset-coloured beach seemed to take much longer than usual. Whether or not he was conscious of her, she was unceasingly conscious of him, and of the current of suspicion that came from him like a cold wind.

'Have you been to the beach yet?' she said.

'No. I've not had time.'

'I suppose not . . . Is Dad really going to buy a boat?'

'He said so. I don't know.'

Silence again. They were walking some way apart, and when they heard a car coming up the lane, they separated, each going to a different side. She wanted to find a way of asking him about the idea that Dad had been in prison, but not yet; she couldn't guess how he'd take it. If only he'd say something on his own instead of letting her start every conversation. If only . . . She could think of a dozen *if onlys* without even trying.

At the car park, almost empty now that the visitors had gone to their bed-and-breakfasts, their rented cottages, their mobile homes, Ginny stopped. Robert drifted to a halt a little way off.

'I'm just trying to work out which way to go,' she said. 'Sometimes they have it over to the right, in the high dunes; sometimes they go the other way. Let's go left.'

She climbed the gate into the field behind the dunes, the field that on its far side bordered the estuary. He joined her hesitantly, as if he wasn't sure it was allowed.

'It's all right,' she said. 'Everyone goes through here. As long as we don't let the sheep out . . .'

'What's that?' he said, pointing to a lichen-crusted slate roof among the dunes.

'That's the church. It's half buried. In the Dark Ages, right, when they had Viking raids and such, there was a monastery on an island out at sea somewhere, and whenever a monk or a priest died here on the mainland, they'd take his body over there to be buried. And the night before they sailed, they'd leave it in this church, all night long. It's called Saint

Cynog's. That's why the village is called Llangynog, see. They open up the church in the holidays and have a service for the people on the beach. Otherwise it just sits here in the sand.'

'Are those graves in there?' he said, looking through the tumbledown lich-gate.

'Yeah. The sand drifts around and covers them up and uncovers them again. It's really really old.'

They clambered up past the tiny church and some way into the dunes, and then Ginny heard music and saw the fire, built in a wide hollow in the sand hills facing the sea. The whole scene was varnished with gold like an old picture of gods and nymphs. And if the ancient gods had barbecues, this was what they'd have looked like: healthy, happy figures drinking, or hauling a log up from the beach, or preparing food for the fire.

But then she looked again and thought, No, they're not gods and nymphs, these are human beings. Gods never changed. It would take someone like Watteau to paint this, with that strange air he had of delicate melancholy under the enjoyment: the sense in the shadows and the colour of the sky that time was passing, that the happy maids and courtiers would change, part, grow old. . . . How could she show that here? If Watteau had painted a barbecue . . . Couldn't draw it; need colour. Oil?

Tempera? With an underglaze of gold . . . It would all be in the colour, precious, fading . . .

The tide was high; it would be fully in by midnight. Rhiannon's kind Peter was there, thrusting a stick into the fire, and suddenly there was Rhiannon herself beside them, bright-eyed, pretty, curious.

'Hi!' she said. 'You must be Robert . . .'

And so they arrived at the barbecue.

Ginny's experience of parties and discos and barbecues was of other people having a good time and of herself watching. When she was younger, she'd thought that that was what a good time was, and she was having it, but in the last couple of years, seeing other girls dancing with boys and holding their hands and being kissed, she'd come to realize that having a good time involved some so far imaginary boy, one who, if not sexy, was at least kind. At the same time she despised her timidity: why didn't *she* take charge? Why didn't she go up to a boy she fancied and . . . And what? That was the question she hadn't worked out the answer to.

But tonight was different. Andy was coming, and the tide was high and the air was warm and the good smell of cooking food came drifting from the fire, and music was playing, and she felt pretty and light and tingling with expectation. So when he did arrive, slipping into the circle round the fire to shouts of 'Andy! Great! Have a drink!' she felt everything was going to come right. And there was Dafydd, his heavy eyes smiling at her, and – she checked – there was Robert, sitting silent on one side of Rhiannon while Peter, looking kind, sat on the other.

'Did you do the ton?' she asked Andy.

'No. Ninety-eight. Harry wanted to get the last two to go round twice, but *Duw*, we'd had enough. *Iesu Grist*, it's bloody hot. Give us a bite to eat. Look, I've got a bottle of wine, lads . . .' He dragged a bottle of Lambrusco out of some capacious pocket and screwed off the top. 'Have a swig.'

Ginny tilted the bottle back. It was sweet and fizzy and cold, and some of it went up her nose and made her sneeze and laugh.

'Don't stick it up your nose,' he said. '*Dreadful* manners. Hey, I was going to bring Gertie, give her a good time, but I thought the excitement would be too much for her. Where's that sausage? Give us a bite.'

'Who's Gertie?' said Eryl. 'You changing your spots, Andy?'

'No spots on me. I'm an Ethiopian.'

'First time I've heard it called that,' said Eryl, but Andy was off on the story of how he came by the smoked salmon. It was quite different from the first version. Dafydd winked and rolled his eyes up at Ginny with a vast secret enjoyment, and she sat clasping her knees beside Andy, the dazzling quick-silver trickster, as he spun one fantastic lie after another. She knew they were lies, knew that the incredible Carlos had probably never existed, but it didn't matter a bit. Listening to Andy was like sitting under a fountain of champagne.

When the bottle of wine was half-finished, she felt dizzy and confident, both at once, and she tugged at his hand and made him get up and dance. It was a slow, romantic soul tune, and several couples were swaying in each other's arms, feet dragging in the soft sand. She faced him for a moment, looked at his dark face directly, and then stepped close and put her arms around his waist.

His body was warm and slender, his arms light around her, and she rested her head on his shoulder and breathed in the complex intoxicating smell of him: the faint remains of cooking and cigarette smoke, the wine, some distant hint of aftershave, and clean sweat. She marvelled at the tension of the smooth muscles of his back, the hollow between them where his spine lay, the way his hips swayed . . . He had no sense of rhythm whatsoever, and such was her state of mind that his lack of it seemed only one more perfection.

She was no longer aware of the other kids, of the fire, the sea, the music, Robert. Everything was Andy; she was obsessed, she was drunk with him, she was in love . . . This was it, love, she was there, it was hers. She moved her head slightly and brushed his neck with her lips, once, twice, and then kissed it gently, lost.

Then someone spoke nearby. There was a muffled laugh. Andy's body tensed at once; she could feel it like electricity. She looked up at his face, dismayed, and saw it grim and cynical.

'Take no notice,' he whispered. 'They're not worth it. They're just a bunch of stupid kids.'

'But what did they *say*?' she whispered back, though she knew. Someone had joked about them, about their being black, some crude racist crap . . . Her *friends*. Andy, sensing her anger, held her tight and didn't let her whirl around to confront them.

'They don't understand,' was all he said.

'But we have to *fight* this, Andy! Not just for us but for everyone! We can't just *give in* . . .'

There was something disconcerting about his response. She couldn't see his face clearly enough, because he had his back to the fire, but she sensed a sadness in him she'd never known before. The music stopped, and they stopped moving, and someone put another tape in. The moment had gone.

They sat down. She was puzzled. There he was, talking to Glyn and Siân and Eryl, making them laugh, accepting a cigarette, offering the wine; and Ginny found herself next to Robert. Something had happened, but she didn't know what it was.

Robert was saying something. She had to ask him to repeat it.

'Who's the gay pair?' he said quietly.

'Gay pair? What're you talking about?'

'Those lads. The one you were dancing with and his mate. What's their names?'

She was bewildered. 'Gay?'

'You know. Homosexual.'

'What d'you *mean*, gay? How can they be – you don't mean Andy and Dafydd? Whatever gave you that stupid idea?'

'Rhiannon told me. Anyway, it's obvious.'

And suddenly it was.

A hundred little meaningless things – comments, looks, jokes – acquired a meaning all at once. And she knew what the whispered voice had said that had made Andy at first tense in her arms and then sad – it was all as clear as water, and she'd been duped again. Everyone else had known, and she hadn't. Rhiannon had known; her best friend. Even Robert had known. It was too much to bear.

With a choking sob, she flung herself up and away from the fire, into the darkness of the dunes. She plunged over the top of the nearest one and fell down into the cool feathery sand on the far side, stumbling and sprawling, and then scrambled up again and struggled through the yielding sand, the pricking marram grass, till she was out of earshot of the group by the fire and their mocking voices, their knowing eyes; and then she sank to her knees and beat her fists into the white unresistant softness all around, the hot tears scalding her hot cheeks.

She'd never felt so humiliated in her life. The worst of it was that she'd made her infatuation for Andy so obvious; she'd flaunted it . . . And *Rhiannon* had known. And Angie had known: *You haven't got a girlfriend, you pillock.* And Eryl, just now: *First time I've heard it called that.* And Stuart: suddenly everything about Stuart became clear. God! Even her father – seeing her with Stuart, and hearing that Stuart was a friend of Andy's, he'd known what that had meant, and said, *Oh, that's all right, then,* meaning *You'll be safe with him . . .*

And she hadn't seen it. Stupid, naive Ginny, the only person in the world who didn't know. She knelt there, her head bowed, the tears soaking into the sand as they fell from her eyes.

Minutes went by, and little by little the crying stopped. She sat up slowly and mopped her face with the skirt. She was alone, and that was how she wanted it.

Very dimly, in the faint starlight, the roof of the old church was visible over the marram-fringed rise in front of her. She sighed a long shaky sigh, stood up and brushed the sand off her skirt, and slowly climbed the slope.

There was a single strand of wire marking the boundary of the churchyard, but the posts were sunk so low in the sand that it was easy to step over it. She slid down among the graves, the leaning tombstones, and made her way to the corner of the church.

In front of her the wide field spread out to the estuary, and beyond it the water, high now the tide was in, gleamed like steel. A cluster of little lights marked the Yacht Club and the railway station, the only sign of human life; and beyond everything else lay the great round hills, dark against the dark sky, immeasurably ancient.

Gradually, as she stood with her right hand on the corner of the tiny church, the shame and the anger cooled down. In the presence of those vast hills, it seemed petty. Maybe the old monks had felt the same about their sorrows, gazing up at that skyline. This church was a thousand years old; such a long time . . . At some time in those thousand years, Ginny thought, someone else must have stood in the same spot, hand on the wall, and looked up at the hills and felt better for it.

At her left hand there was a slate-covered tomb the size and height of a table, a big dark box half covered in sand. The light grains against the black surface reminded her of something. She brushed the top clear and, taking a handful of sand, let it trickle through her fingers on to the slate.

After a little practice she found she could draw a strong clear line.

She was thinking of what Stuart had told her about the *vevers*, those magic figures the voodoo priest would trace in flour on the ground to evoke the *loa*, the gods. Carefully she drew the outline of a heart, pierced by a sword, with lacy fronds and tendrils extending from the top and bottom. In the ghostly starlight she could see it clearly. It was the *vever* of Erzulie, the tragic goddess of love, whose visitations were brief and ended in weeping, but who brought beauty with her, and grace, and laughter – tragic things, because they lasted so short a time and then died.

When it was nearly finished she stood back and looked at it. The handle of the sword was too large; she brushed it away and corrected it. She did the same for one of the tendrils at the foot, which didn't balance the one on the other side. Then it was done.

She straightened her back stiffly, conscious that she'd made a decision of some kind. She felt very tired and oddly happy, and her mind was filled with a tangle of thoughts: *I can see in the dark. I can't see so well in the daylight, can't see the obvious things like Andy being gay, but that doesn't matter because I can see in the dark. I can understand mysteries. Like the broken bridge. I know the truth of that, because I'm the baby, I'm the father, I'm the thief. And I understand the old monks who built this church, and Erzulie, I understand her, and the hills too, I can hear what they're saying to me. And African-ness. I'm beginning to understand being black. And my mother. Something happened when I was born, I know it did. I'm going to find out. I'm going to find her paintings . . . They're not going to hide things from me. They're so stupid! They hide them in the* dark! *If they hid them in the light I'd never see them, but the dark is where I live, like Maman. I'm an artist, I'm a sorceress, I'm at home there . . . So whatever it is you concealed, Dad, you made a mistake. I'm going to find it. And then I'll paint the truth . . .*

She found herself wandering through the field, her feet wet in the dew, her head ringing.

There was a figure sitting on the gate by the car park.

'Robert?' she said.

He got down on the other side.

'Thought I'd better wait for you,' he said.

'No need. But thanks.'

She climbed the gate, and they began to walk up the lane. She was immensely tired. For the first time she thought what it all must mean to him: his mother had died only a week ago, and this stranger, his unknown sister, takes him to a barbecue and involves him in her own little emotional dramas. She wanted to apologize, but it was more comfortable being silent; at least they weren't hostile any more.

Almost the last thing she realized that night came to her as she was getting into bed. Holding Andy in her arms, the voice, her anger, his sadness . . . He was sad for her, because he'd seen her mistake and known he could do nothing about it. She felt very fond of him, fond of Dafydd. It wasn't their fault, after all. That things could be like that . . . How strange. How *strange*. It was like losing a twenty-pound note but then seeing a new colour.

Her very last thought concerned Joe Chicago, as

she realized the meaning of his connection with Andy. Things were fitting into place. Maman, the broken bridge . . . It was beginning to make sense. But there was a lot more to find out yet. She went to sleep almost at once.

Chapter Ten

The only thing to do

Ginny wasn't sure what she was going to say to Rhiannon, so it was a good thing the next day was Sunday, when she didn't go to the Dragon. Instead, after lunch (difficult, with Dad trying to be cheerful and fatherly and Robert being grim and silent), she went off on her own and caught the train to Porthafon.

At the corner of Jubilee Terrace she almost turned back, because outside Rhiannon's sister's house there was a man washing a car – obviously Helen's husband. Washing cars was discouraged if not actually forbidden because of the water shortage, so getting it clean was clearly very important to him. He was a neat, trim little man with hairy arms and the famous neat moustache, and he looked at her with open curiosity as she went past him and rang the doorbell.

Helen answered it seconds before her husband got there, chamois cloth dripping in his hand.

'Ginny . . . Come in.'

A quick, hostile glance at him, and she closed the door behind them, shutting him out.

'Come on through. I'm in the garden,' she said.

Ginny had forgotten how definite she was, how clear and decisive and un-Rhiannon-like. They sat down on the little patch of grass, with children playing on a swing next door and a man on the opposite side of the fence dozing under a newspaper. It felt very open compared to her back garden; she imagined everyone would be listening.

'I've heard about your brother,' Helen said.

'From Rhiannon? Or from Dad?'

Helen hesitated. 'Both,' she said.

'Do you see Dad a lot, then?'

'Well . . . quite often.'

She looked frankly at Ginny, as if inviting her to ask more. But Ginny didn't want to, yet.

'So. What's this brother like?' Helen said.

'Difficult. I have to keep telling myself he's my brother, or I wouldn't believe it. Half-brother. And that his mum only died last week. It's no wonder he's unhappy. And what he thinks of us, God knows. I try and ask about his mother . . . Actually I don't any more, 'cause he got angry, but I was just so curious, I wanted to *know*. And Dad won't tell me . . .'

'Why won't he?'

'He just clams up. He won't say anything except stupid vague answers that don't mean anything. I want to know about my mother, for instance. I thought they were married, but they weren't; he was married to Robert's mother. Did you know that?'

Helen nodded, looking careful.

'What else has he told you, then?'

Helen blew out her cheeks and ran a hand through her hair. 'It's not easy . . .'

Ginny felt a flash of anger. 'What d'you mean, it's not easy? What d'you think it's like for me? There's everyone knowing more about me than I do myself – what d'you think that's like?'

Helen looked down. Ginny pressed on recklessly: 'Are you having an affair with Dad?'

'*What?* Ginny, I can't answer—'

'Is that what it is? You can tell me, for God's sake! I don't *mind* or anything! I mean, *are* you?'

'Have you asked him?'

'Yes,' said Ginny, staring at her flatly.

'And? What did he say?'

'He said no, of course not, what a stupid idea.'

'Well, then . . .'

'But he's a liar, isn't he? He lied about my mother. He might be lying about this. That's why I'm asking you.'

Helen's eyes were closed. Ginny was hating herself for this, but now she'd started, she couldn't stop.

'Ginny,' said Helen, 'I like your father very much, but I can't answer questions like that. Let me talk to him—'

She stopped, and Ginny looked around. Benny was watching from the kitchen doorway.

'All right?' he said, as if Ginny had been starting a fight.

'Yes, thank you,' said Helen coldly.

'Who's this, then?' he said, smiling at Ginny.

'Ginny. She's a friend of Rhiannon's.'

'I'd better go,' said Ginny, thinking that they'd never be able to talk with him there.

'No, don't. Wait a minute, I'll come with you,' said Helen, getting up.

Ginny pushed past Benny in the kitchen doorway, not looking at him, smelling his pungent aftershave.

'Let's go down to the Locker,' said Helen. 'Have a coffee and a doughnut or something.'

Davy Jones's Locker was a café on the harbour-front, all hung about with lobster pots and fishing nets and glass floats, and someone had painted mermaids and pirate wrecks on the walls. The owner was a big careless cheerful man with one leg, who sometimes wore a pirate-style striped jersey and stumped about on a wooden peg like Long John Silver. The whole thing was tacky, but Ginny liked the wooden booths and the smell of fresh coffee, which came in chunky earthenware mugs that didn't balance properly on the saucers.

'Have some carrot cake,' said Helen. 'Help you see in the dark.'

Ginny decided that she liked her a lot.

'I'm sorry I said that about Dad,' she said. 'I didn't really ask him at all. I couldn't, even if I wanted to. But I'm just so confused, what with Robert and all, I don't know anything. And last night . . . There was this boy, right . . .'

She told Helen about Andy, about how she'd felt, about what had happened. Helen listened with all Rhiannon's intense interest but with a lot more sympathy.

'It's funny, though,' Ginny said. 'I don't feel cross or anything. It's just embarrassing, really. The real thing about it is Joe Chicago, how it links up with him. You know the story of the broken bridge?'

'No. What's that?'

'You *don't*? I thought that was just one more of the things everyone knew but me. A long time ago there was a man with his daughter, a baby, driving up Gwynant way, and it was a winter night, and the car crashed into the bridge. They weren't hurt or anything. The man had a warm kind of fur-lined leather jacket, and he wrapped me up in it and went for help. But while he was gone someone stole the jacket and the baby died, just froze to death. And *I* reckon that the person who did it was Joe Chicago, and that's the same jacket, the one he wears. Now, if he knew my dad was in prison, OK, then Dad's connected with that story in the same way. So I really need to find out all I can.'

'Why did you say *me?*'

'Me?'

'You said *he wrapped me up in it.* Instead of *the baby.*'

'I didn't, did I? Did I really?'

Helen nodded and sipped her coffee. 'It's a Freudian slip,' she said.

'What's that?'

'It means it's what you really think. Your unconscious mind speaking for you.'

'But I don't think... It wouldn't make sense anyway, 'cause I'm not dead, am I?'

'No. Probably just a slip of the tongue.'

Ginny slid further into the corner of the booth, pulled her feet up on the wooden seat, and hugged her knees, staring unseeingly at the fishing net spread out on the opposite wall.

'Rhiannon said that Joe Chicago knows your husband,' she said.

'Yeah,' said Helen after a second or two.

'Do *you* know him?'

'He's been to the house a few times.'

'He's involved with that boy I told you about. Andy. I think he's blackmailing him or something. And I think I know why now, after last night. D'you think he really knows my dad?'

'I don't know . . . I don't know. The thing is that Benny's so bloody jealous of everything, everyone, and he knows I've seen your dad once or twice . . . He might have made that up. To try and put me off, see. I never heard it from Joe himself, only from Benny.'

'So it might not be true?'

'Or it might.'

They were silent. Helen pushed the plate of cake towards Ginny, who shook her head.

'I can already see in the dark,' she said.

They sat there a little while longer and then went out to the harbour and sat looking at the cottages, the old slate warehouse that was now an Industrial Heritage Museum, the amusement arcade. It was another hot day. Helen was fanning herself with her straw hat.

'Helen, does he ever talk about my mother?'

Ginny asked. 'Because I want to find her paintings, you see. I can't understand why he didn't keep them.'

'Well . . . I couldn't say, really. Listen, now. This is going to sound stupid, but did you ever think that maybe your mam was still alive?'

Ginny blinked with astonishment. How ridiculous!

'Of course she's not,' she said scornfully. 'I'd know if she was alive, wouldn't I?'

'How, though?'

'I'd have heard of her. She'd be a famous painter. Anyway, I *know* she's not alive. She'd never have left me if she was. It's out of the question.'

She was a little angry that Helen could even consider it possible. They sat in silence for a while, and Ginny began to wonder why she'd come, what this woman had to do with her, why she'd wasted her time. Well, she'd leave in a minute, as soon as she found a way of saying goodbye.

But Helen said, 'Why are you so interested in Joe Chicago?'

'I told you. Because of the broken bridge.'

'Suppose you found out it *was* him: what would you do?'

'What would I do? Well, I'd be able to make him

leave Andy alone, for a start. And . . . make him tell me about Dad.'

Before she said the words the idea hadn't existed, but now that it did, she knew it was absolutely right. She felt a little thrill of certainty.

'Does he come to your house often?' she said.

'Whenever Benny brings him, I suppose. I don't take much notice. I'm not very close to Benny these days. I don't know what they've got in common anyway. I think Benny's afraid of him. He's just trying to show he's tough, going around with a thug.'

'Helen, could you help me?'

'Help you talk to Joe Chicago?'

'Yeah. Could you?' She was sitting forward on the wooden bench, twisted to look Helen in the face, and Helen, her straw hat low over her eyes, was leaning back languidly in the heat, looking tired.

'*Please?*' Ginny said.

'I think you're crazy. He's a horrible swine, he's hateful, you don't want to talk to him . . . What makes you think he'll tell you the truth anyway?'

'I'll make him,' said Ginny. 'I will. Me and Baron Samedi, we'll make him.'

'You and who?'

'My voodoo friend. No; no one – I don't mean it. Just me.'

'But what are you . . .?'

'I just need to be alone with him for a few minutes, Helen. I just want to ask him. *Please* . . . When he comes to your house next time, can you let me know? I'll get someone to bring me.'

Helen pursed her lips. Then she shrugged.

'Well, it can't do much harm, I suppose . . . Are you going to tell your dad?'

'No! Course not.'

'And . . . are you going to tell him you've been to see me?'

She'd put her sunglasses on; Ginny couldn't read her expression.

'No,' she said. 'If he's got secrets from me, I can have secrets from him. I can't talk to him any more, not now Robert's here. We're never alone. Anyway, I don't trust him.'

'You should.'

'I can't. I'm on my own now.'

'No, you're not,' said Helen unconvincingly.

'I am.'

'But how was I supposed to know?' said Rhiannon the following afternoon. 'Know you didn't know, I mean, stupid. Everyone's always known. That's why he left home, 'cause his parents chucked him out for it. I mean, it was such an *obvious* thing. That's why you've got nothing to worry about.'

'Explain,' said Ginny coldly.

'No one'll think you didn't know. They'll think you were dancing with him just as a friend, kind of thing.'

'Oh, yeah?'

'Oh bloody yeah.'

'And what about when I ran off into the dunes? I thought they were all laughing at me.'

'You don't suppose anyone noticed anything by that stage, girl? I certainly didn't. I was in the second degree of bliss,' she said with a comic smugness. 'That's a technical term.'

'The second degree of bliss . . .' Ginny said scornfully, but she couldn't help smiling. 'I suppose Peter took you there, did he? And how many degrees of bliss are there?'

'Judging by that one, I reckon about seven hundred. Still, it's a start. Hey, someone's waving at you.'

They were sitting on the old wooden jetty outside the Yacht Club. Ginny looked where Rhiannon was pointing.

'That's Stuart,' she said, waving back.

'Who he?'

'A friend of Andy's. Yes,' she said, answering the

174

question in Rhiannon's raised eyebrows. 'And I didn't know before, no. But he's nice. Let's go and say hello.'

They stood up, bare feet on the hot planks, and took the path along by the railway bridge to the ladder that led to Stuart's house. He was sitting on the roof, sunbathing. Rhiannon drew in her breath as she saw him.

'What a *waste*,' she said quietly, climbing the ladder just behind Ginny.

'I'll tell him,' Ginny said.

When she came face-to-face with Stuart again, Ginny felt herself wondering what did it *mean*, being gay? What did they *do*? Had he kissed Andy, for instance?

'Hi,' he said. 'I've got something for you. Hello,' he added to Rhiannon.

'This is Rhiannon,' Ginny said. 'My social secretary.'

'I'm Stuart,' he said. 'I haven't got one of those, I'm afraid; you have to deal with me directly. How's things?'

'Mixed,' said Ginny, sitting down beside him on the decking of the roof. Rhiannon sat down too, and Ginny saw with pleasure that her friend, for once, was shy. Stuart was wearing the smallest possible swimming costume, and his body, as far as she could judge male bodies, could probably take you to the five hundredth degree of bliss merely by being looked at. 'Did I have a brother when I saw you last? I can't remember.'

'You didn't mention him. Has he just appeared?'

'That's him down there, in the boat with my dad. Dad's the one with the beard.'

Stuart looked across the water to the edge of the jetty, two hundred yards away, where the apparent owner of the boat was demonstrating how to do something nautical with the sail. Dad was looking brisk and keen, and Robert was sitting in the stern, staring down into the water.

'He doesn't look very happy,' said Stuart.

'No. Well, he's probably not . . . How are you, then?'

'Roasting. I thought it was supposed to rain all the time here.'

'Well, it's the end of the world. Everything's going strange. What's this thing you've got for me?'

'A magazine. It's downstairs on the table.'

'What is it? What magazine?'

'Well, you're interested in art; I thought you'd like it. Read it carefully. Oh, and I want to see some of your pictures. Is she any good?' he asked Rhiannon.

'Yeah, brilliant,' said Rhiannon. She *was* shy, Ginny thought gleefully.

'D'you ever go to the Yacht Club?' she asked.

'Yes. I've been several times. Why?'

'Well, next Saturday, you've got to go three times. They want to do the ton – that's a hundred dinners. They got up to ninety-eight last Saturday, so if you have three meals, they might make it next time.'

'Or bring two friends,' said Stuart.

'Yeah, that'd do . . .'

They stayed on his roof for half an hour, watching Dad and Robert in the little boat, gossiping, joking. Rhiannon hardly spoke, but Ginny was completely at her ease, laughing and flirting in a way she knew she could never have done with a boy her own age, or someone who wasn't gay. She found herself thinking that it would be an ideal relationship, all easy, all happy, all surface. All sun, all skin. But that wasn't enough now.

'Don't forget that magazine,' Stuart called as they left. 'Come and see me again.'

'Yeah, we will,' said Ginny.

The magazine on the table was thick and glossy and called *Modern Painters*. Well, that's nice, she thought. I'll read it tonight.

*

177

And so she did; but it wasn't until some days later that she saw why he'd given it to her. There was just so much of it – articles on painters she'd never heard of, articles on painters she had heard of, an article by an English painter explaining why an American painter wasn't as good as everyone had thought, an article by a Scottish painter explaining why a Spanish painter was better than anyone had thought, articles by critics attacking other critics – pages and pages of it, and Ginny read it all avidly, because this was her world now, these were her people. And the illustrations were beautiful.

But she hadn't seen Andy since the barbecue, and something was weighing on her mind. Should she pretend nothing had happened? Should they talk about it? In the end, it was easy. She was sitting moodily on the beach on Tuesday afternoon, and suddenly there he was, beside her, holding out an ice cream.

'What's the matter? You wanted chocolate? Tough. You got this.'

She took it, and he stroked the back of her neck for an awkward second. It was the only awkward action she'd ever known him to perform, and she knew exactly what it meant: it was an acknowledgement, and a consolation, and an apology, and she realized with a little rush of relief that the ideal relationship she'd imagined while talking to Stuart already existed between her and Andy.

'Listen,' she said, 'you know Joe Chicago?'

'What about him?'

'Where did he get that jacket from? His leather jacket.'

'Oh, you heard that story, have you?'

Her skin prickled. 'What story?'

'He nicked it. That's what I heard. There was a plane that crashed in the hills, and he went up and took it off the dead pilot. That's what he likes to tell people. Wants to make himself sound really hard. Big pillock.'

'A plane . . . Wow. How things change. You know he's friendly with Rhiannon's sister's husband?'

'Has she got a sister? God, the whole world's coming out in siblings. Tell me more . . .'

It felt good to have him back. No, it felt better, because now both of them knew what their relationship was, and if she had to put a name to it, it would have been the one he'd just used: they were siblings, kindred, blood relatives.

She felt far more his sister than Robert's. It wasn't getting any easier at home; Dad tried to get them to talk at mealtimes, but since the things they had in common were the things that neither Dad nor Robert wanted to talk about, conversation faltered.

They couldn't even talk about school. Robert had just finished his GCSEs, as she'd done, but she had no idea what he was intending to study next. She didn't even know if he was clever. What he seemed mostly was grim and angry.

And Ginny understood, or tried to, but she could find nothing to say to him; and so while she hung around with Rhiannon or with Andy and Dafydd, and worked in the Dragon and the Yacht Club, Robert drifted about alone on long walks in the hills; and while he sat silently with Dad in front of the TV, she spent the evenings at her drawing table, pencilling the story picture of the broken bridge.

On Thursday night she'd got it laid out as she wanted it, ready to be inked. It was midnight when she finished, and she was tempted to go on, to ink just the first frame, to lay the pure Indian black on the crisp white Bristol board; but she knew that her eyes were tired and her hand was cramped, and she didn't want to risk spoiling it. Instead she had a shower and went to bed. The window was open; it was too hot for pyjamas, and even her bedside lamp, shining on *Modern Painters*, was uncomfortably warm. Eyelids drooping, she lay flicking through the magazine before falling asleep.

And suddenly she found herself frozen. A shiver, a chill, made her skin crawl, and she realized her heart was racing as she tried to work out what had caused it: someone prowling outside? A ghost? What?

It was the magazine. She sat up and looked.

A gallery in Liverpool was advertising an exhibition called *Les Mystères: Haitian Painting of the Past Twenty Years*, and one of the painters was Anielle Baptiste.

She clenched her fists, alive with triumph. So the pictures *had* survived! And that was why Stuart had given her the magazine! When was it opening, this exhibition? On Tuesday next, for a month, at L'Ouverture Gallery in Sandeman Street . . .

She couldn't lie still; she was far too excited to sleep now. Wide awake, grinning helplessly, she switched on the work light over her drawing table, uncapped the ink, and choosing her finest brush, began to work on *The Broken Bridge*.

Chapter Eleven
Baron Samedi

By this time, Ginny was in a strange state of mind, with three things pressing equally on her attention: her painting of the broken bridge; her mother's pictures, and wondering what they'd be like, and keeping the news of them secret; and the crazy quest to get the truth out of Joe Chicago. She looked haunted, absentminded, obsessed, anything but happy – though if anyone had asked her whether she was unhappy, she wouldn't have known what they were talking about. She was only aware that she was busy. And this, she dimly realized, was a state of mind as much hers as art, as seeing in the dark. It was the place where she was at home.

On Saturday at the Dragon, Rhiannon said (quietly, because Mr Calvert was just outside the door), 'Helen rang this morning with a message for you. She said she couldn't ring your house in case your dad found out. Hey, is she having an affair with him? I bet she is. I would, if I was married to Benny. But she won't say—'

'What's the *message?*' Ginny said.

'Oh. Right. Yeah. She said Joe Chicago will be there tonight. Ginny, what's going *on?* Why's she telling you that?'

'It's a secret code. It means something different.'

'Oh, all right then, don't tell me. I just won't tell you about Robert.'

'What about Robert?' said Ginny, though she didn't care. It wouldn't have surprised her at all if Rhiannon was interested in him. In fact, the only person who would have been surprised was Peter.

But to satisfy Rhiannon's curiosity, she said, 'I'm having a bet with Andy, that's all. I want to find out something from Joe Chicago. And I told Helen, and she's going to help me.'

'He'll kill you,' said Rhiannon pleasurably. 'With his bare hands. He's a sadist, you know. He indulges in unspeakable atrocities. You're taking your life in your hands, girl . . .'

The biggest problem was how to get back. If she left the Yacht Club exactly on time, she'd just catch the one bus that went that way on Saturdays, but there was no bus back, and no trains, either.

Well, ask, she told herself, and went down to the trailer to look for Dafydd.

He groaned. 'I'm not getting involved with Joe

Chicago,' he said. 'Nor should you. Is this Andy's idea?'

'No. It's all mine. You wouldn't have to get involved anyway, just be somewhere I can find you. And then drive me home. I'll pay for the petrol.'

'Forget the petrol. I can fill the tank any time. Well, I suppose so. All right. I think you're going round the bend, I really do. What time d'you reckon you'll want to come home?'

Dad suggested optimistically at teatime that maybe they could all go out and see a film and have a pizza that evening. Ginny wasn't aware of the look of contempt that passed over her face and would have been horrified if she realized he'd noticed; but they were communicating so little these days that she'd lost the habit of looking for his response to things. She told him that she was going out, and that she'd be back at eleven, and then forgot about him.

The Yacht Club was gearing up to do the ton. Angie Lime had made sure the suppliers had delivered all the vegetables they were likely to need; the bar was freshly stocked; all the staff were concentrating, flexing their muscles, thinking ahead. It was a heady atmosphere, and Ginny half wished she could stay and be part of it.

But she hurried away, wishing them luck, and

then ran up to the main road so as not to miss the bus. When it came, she sat in the front seat, the evening sun full in her face, and felt an agreeable tension prickling its way along her nerves, like stage fright. In her jeans and trainers and dark T-shirt, she felt light, athletic, ready to run and fight.

At Porthafon she got out by the harbour and wandered along past Davy Jones's Locker, wondering whether to go in and have some coffee, but the place was full of holiday-makers eating hamburgers. She moved on. The harbour was lively, with its cafés and pubs and the amusement arcade, but the rest of the town was very quiet. It was beginning to get dark as she turned into Jubilee Terrace. The light was on in the front room of Helen's house, but Ginny couldn't see anyone. Helen opened the door at once when she rang the bell.

'Come in, quick,' she said, 'before they see you . . .'

Ginny hastened into the hall, and Helen shut the door quickly.

'They've gone to the pub to get some beer,' she said.

'Him and Benny. They're going to play cards or something. You haven't seen him close to, have you? He's frightening. You can't imagine.'

'I have seen him,' Ginny said. 'You don't have to do anything. Just leave it to me.'

'But what are *you* going to do?'

'I don't know! I'll think of something. I just want to talk to him on his own . . .'

They were standing in the tidy little hall, talking urgently, the light shining directly down on them. Suddenly Helen seized Ginny's arm.

'They're here!' she whispered, and Ginny heard voices outside. 'Get upstairs! Go on – quick!'

Ginny ran up the narrow stairs as a key turned in the lock. She hesitated on the landing, crouching low in the dark to peer down at Benny and Joe and two other men, all crowding in. They were speaking Welsh; Helen said something sharp to Benny, and Joe said something back that made the other men laugh. Ginny could see Benny's face, and saw that it was more important to him to seem good to these men than to stick up for Helen, and then she understood all Helen's contempt.

The men shoved their way into the front room. Ginny heard the snapping of aluminium can pulls, the sudden blare of the TV, quickly turned down. Then Helen was on her way upstairs.

'Come in here,' she whispered to Ginny, pushing open a door at the top of the stairs that led into a stuffy little spare bedroom overlooking the garden.

She didn't turn the light on. They sat on the bed and spoke quietly.

'What are they doing?' Ginny asked.

'Drinking. They'll play cards till they think I've gone to bed, and then they'll watch a dirty video. Benny gets them from someone in town – I saw it in his shopping bag. God, he thinks I'm a fool.'

'What does Joe do? Does he sleep here?'

'I wouldn't dare sleep with him in the house. No, he's got a council house somewhere; he always goes home. Listen, why don't you give up the idea, for God's sake? You don't know what he might do . . .'

'I'll just wait here. Sooner or later he'll come up to the bathroom or something. Is the front door locked?'

'Well, it's on the latch – a Yale lock. What d'you mean?'

'Can you fix the latch so I just have to pull it open? You know, instead of having to turn the handle, if I want to run out in a hurry?'

'I could, but listen, I'm frightened now. I'm worried what he'll do to me if—'

She stopped. Heavy footsteps came up the stairs; a man pissed loudly into the lavatory bowl and didn't flush it or wash his hands before going down again. Fastidious Helen made a face.

'Was that him, d'you think?' Ginny said.

'Might have been. They're all horrible, *ach y fi*, and the worst is Benny . . .'

'I saw him when Joe said that to you.'

'I can't stay with him, Ginny; there's no reason to. He treats me like shit; he spends all his time sucking up to thugs like Joe . . .'

She was crying, silently but passionately, and then she turned to throw herself on the pillow, her sobs heaving her shoulders. Ginny felt helpless. She put her hand on Helen's back, but Helen didn't seem to feel it. Ginny had never seen a grown woman cry before; it was like a force of nature, Erzulie again: here on this narrow bed in this dark and stuffy room, the goddess was weeping. Ginny was awed by the power and intensity of it, and simultaneously she imagined painting the scene: the two of them in the light coming from the crack under the door, the dim room, Helen's cloud of dark hair, her own face baffled and anxious, her tentative hand. She found herself sketching it in her mind and moved her right leg to improve the balance of the composition – and then cursed her own selfishness. Art was a *disease*, to make you more concerned about pictorial values than about someone else's unhappiness.

Presently Helen sat up slowly and dried her eyes. She wouldn't look at Ginny.

'I'll go and put the door on the latch,' she said. 'Then I'm going to bed.'

With a deep, trembling sigh, she stood up and went out. Ginny heard her descend the stairs, heard the kitchen door open and close, heard laughter from the front room, heard Helen coming up the stairs again, heard her bedroom door close.

Then, for the first time, with part of her mind she wondered what she was doing. If she had any sense she'd go quietly downstairs and leave the house, and wait for Dafydd, and forget all about the broken bridge.

But another part of her mind said: *Stick to it, I'm right, this is desperately important, I've got to find out the truth* . . .

And the second voice won.

She opened the bedroom door a crack, so that she could just see the top of the stairs, and sat down on the floor to wait.

The sound of voices and the music from some TV show came from the front room. Occasionally a car drove past, its headlights sweeping across the ceiling of the landing. There was nothing from Helen's room but silence. Ginny had the feeling that she'd locked her door.

She sat back more comfortably, so that her legs wouldn't get cramped. A long time went by. Benny came up and went to the bathroom, tried Helen's door, made a face, and went down again. A little later, another man came up to visit the bathroom. Ginny could smell the beer as he went past the door. *Drink more,* she thought. *Go on, drink lots.*

And finally Joe Chicago himself came up the stairs. She heard his voice in the downstairs hall and kept pressed against the wall in the dark as the heavy steps came up the staircase and along the landing, as the thunderous splashing came from the bathroom.

Ginny stood up slowly. Her heart was thumping so hard it hurt. She heard him come out of the bathroom and pulled open the bedroom door to face him.

He stopped in surprise.

He was only a yard or so away. She'd forgotten how big he was, that monstrous bull-like mass, that bloated head. His red-rimmed eyes glared at her hotly.

Before he could speak she put a finger to her lips and stood aside, beckoning him into the dark bedroom. Slowly, like a wary animal, he walked in, and then she shut the door, committing herself to the dark with him.

'What d'you want?' he said after a second.

She could sense him beside her. She could smell him, the gross bulk of him, and into her mind came a picture of the broken bridge, the car, the abandoned baby.

Then something happened to Ginny.

She felt a blow inside her head, and then *she* was thrust aside, and there was someone in there with her. She struggled briefly against it, feeling dizzy and terrified, but it was no good: he was stronger by far. He was deadly and powerful and godlike: dark glasses, a top hat, a ragged coat: skeletons, corpses: Baron Samedi . . . She'd boasted that he'd help her, and here he was, and the room was drenched with fear, terrible panic fear.

She felt Joe Chicago take a step backward: he was afraid too.

She whispered, 'Give me your jacket.'

And it wasn't her voice. It was nasal, mocking, horrible; it spoke out of graves and cemeteries, out of the land of death.

'Give me your jacket,' it said again.

The jacket? Ginny was helpless. What did Baron Samedi want the jacket for? There was nothing she could do except hold on faintly and watch; he was out of control. She'd never been so frightened in her life.

Joe was cowering against the wall. 'What for? Who are you? What the bloody hell d'you want with me?'

In the dim light through the window, she could see the glitter of his red-rimmed eyes in a bulk of shadow.

'You've got to give it to me,' she found herself saying. 'You know why? You know what'll happen if you don't?' The fear was constricting her throat. She was losing altogether any sense of who she was. Ginny, that little identity so permanent and important a minute ago, was fading and vanishing, and there was the god in her place, the *loa*, Baron Samedi, mighty and terrible. 'You know what'll happen if you don't?' said his voice, a singsong of death. 'The spirits will get you, Joe. The ghosts will get you. The baby's ghost. The baby in the car. You remember that, Joe? The little baby freezing in the car? She wants the jacket back. She's been waiting long enough. Her ghost is here in the room with us. She's only an arm's length away from your heart, she's going to reach for it with her icy hands and take hold of it and squeeze hard, and you'll feel a pain in all your limbs, you'll feel the ice crushing your heart, you'll feel everything freezing inside you—'

'Shut up!' he bellowed. 'Shut your bloody mouth, bitch!' and then she was Ginny again and she thought: *Oh, thank God he's broken the spell. What was I doing, what was happening?*

And then he tore off the jacket and flung it at her feet and turned away. 'Go on! Go on! Take it! You want it, take the bloody thing! Leave me alone!'

And in the stale darkness of the little room she stooped and picked it up, and then she was out of the room and down the stairs and away, breathing the clean air of the night, tears running down her cheeks.

She didn't stop till she reached the car park by the harbour, where she was going to meet Dafydd. The lights in Davy Jones's Locker, the voices from the pub, music from one of the boats in the harbour where they were having a party – it was all real, and she didn't believe any of it.

Clutching the bulky jacket to her chest, she sat on the low wall and tried to work out what had happened, trembling in the mist of fear that still clung around her. Out of nowhere a god had come into her head. It was what happened in voodoo, Stuart had said; the gods came down and possessed the worshippers. It was her fault: she'd asked for it. *I'll make him. Me and Baron Samedi, we'll make him . . .* He'd heard, and he'd come.

And she was still half in his world, half in a moonlit cemetery, shivering as the ragged top-hatted figure in the dark glasses grinned and jested with her. He'd come to help her. But did she want help like that? What price would she have to pay?

And the jacket – that had been the *loa's* idea. She hadn't had the slightest notion about that; she'd been as surprised as Joe. What on earth was she going to do with it?

She heard the familiar rattle of Dafydd's car and saw it stopping on the far side. She stood up and waved, and then stepped over the wall and made her way across.

'OK?' he said. 'What you got there? You nicked his jacket?'

She nodded and got in beside him. He had the top down, and his greasy hair was all swept back by the wind. He moved off quickly; a left turn, another left, a roundabout, and then there was nothing but the level crossing and the toll bridge and then the long flat road home under the bright moon.

'You happy now?' said Dafydd after a mile.

'What?' She hadn't heard him. It was cold in the open-topped car, with only her T-shirt on and the sweat drying on her arms and breast. She pulled the jacket around her shoulders and shrugged herself into its warmth.

Chapter Twelve
A journey

The jacket was dark brown, cracked and stained, with a heavy zipper and a high collar and a thick sheepskin lining. A greasy, barely legible label over the inside breast pocket said that it had been made by Schwartz Brothers of Chicago. It could have been a flying jacket, as Andy's version of the story said; it would certainly have been the ideal thing to wrap a baby in to keep it warm on a winter's night.

On Sunday morning, Ginny pored over it for hours. She wrapped it around her pillow and drew it from every angle; she turned the pockets inside out, finding nothing but a couple of old bus tickets; and she wondered what on earth she was going to do with it. What did Baron Samedi want it for? The idea came to her of burning it, taking it up to Gwynant on a winter's night and setting fire to it, as a sacrifice to propitiate the spirit of the lost dead child.

It was all confused in her mind with the slip she'd made when she was talking to Helen: *He wrapped me up in it.* If she was the baby, what did that make the jacket? Her mother?

And in the meantime, she must keep away from Joe Chicago. She still wasn't entirely sure what had happened in the spare room at Jubilee Terrace; it had been terrifying to feel her own personality shrinking and disappearing, brushed aside so easily by something stronger and far more ancient. Now she couldn't think which would be worse: to face Joe Chicago on her own, or to face him with that god in her head. Either way would be horrible. Like Andy, she'd just have to keep away from him.

Later that day, she quarrelled with Robert.

It was Dad who was the cause of it, because Ginny and Robert would never have spoken to each other if he hadn't suggested that they all go out in the boat he'd just bought. The two of them had reached a silent accommodation by this time; half-unconsciously they'd manoeuvred themselves into a position where the first one to make a friendly approach would have admitted being the weaker, so now they ignored each other as much as possible, which was at least a way of getting by.

But when, after lunch, Dad, sounding a little desperate, suggested a trip in the boat, Robert rolled his eyes and groaned. Ginny noticed, and a savage instinct made her want to attack him at once; but she held back, and said, 'No, thanks, Dad. I was going to see Rhiannon this afternoon. She'll be expecting me.'

'Bring her too,' he said.

'Not this time. She'll be seasick or something stupid. Next time, I promise.'

So he went off alone, leaving Ginny and Robert together. As soon as Dad had left, she turned on Robert like a tiger.

'You don't have to be so bloody rude, rolling your eyes like that. He's only doing it for you – don't you realize that?'

They were in the garden, he in the hammock as usual, she standing tensely nearby. He looked up from his book – a cold look, direct, fully awake, charged.

'What about you last night?'

'What about me?' Ginny didn't know what he could mean. 'We're not talking about me. We're talking about him and what he's trying to do.'

'Oh, he's a saint, is he? He's like you, is he? He's perfect?'

'What's that supposed to mean?'

'It means stop bloody patronizing me and telling me how to behave.'

'Someone needs to.'

'Why? You think I've got worse manners than you, you snooty bitch? You've been looking down your nose at me ever since I came.'

'I have not!'

'You don't think you have, no, probably not. It's unconscious. You're so sure of how superior you are, it comes off you like a stink, you know that?'

If she hadn't been holding herself in, tense and quivering, she'd have gasped. Instead she flared back, 'So lying about in the hammock expecting people to wait on you hand and foot, so never lifting a finger to help get the food or wash the dishes, that makes you a *democrat* or something, does it? And as for being superior, you're so bloody superior we're not even allowed to know about your mother; she's hidden in mystery; we're all supposed to *bow* or something—'

'My mother?' He was sitting up now, his feet on the ground on either side keeping the hammock still. 'You want to know something about my mother? All right, I'll tell you this: she was *clean*, she was *proud*, you could come into our house and never find dirty cups and plates lying about, dust all over everything, dirty windows, a filthy kitchen – God, I hate eating what comes out of the oven in there, it's so thick with filth and grease. She was strong, my mother, she had principles, that's why

198

she wouldn't have anything to do with *him* after he went sniffing round *your* mother. I bet she was a—'

'Don't you *dare* say anything about her! You don't know *anything*! Cleaning the oven? Washing the windows? Christ, is that all you think women are for? You do, don't you! She probably brought you up like that! She probably waited on you like a servant, just because you were a *boy*; she probably had nothing else in her head but running round after you, picking up your dirty socks, being a *slave* . . . Pathetic. At least my mother was an artist. At least she *thought* about things. She had a talent, she had a gift—'

'That's just what I mean, isn't it? There you go again, looking down on people! Your mum the great artist – so bloody what? Does that make anyone a better person, being a pissy *artist*? Does it? If you go about thinking that . . . well, Christ, it's no wonder everyone thinks you're such a snob, talking down to them—'

'What? *What*? Who thinks I'm a snob?'

'All your friends. Can't you tell? No, you probably can't; you're too high and mighty. Everyone else just looks small to you, probably, they're *amusing* in their little way, or *picturesque*, or *pitiful*, so you patronize them or give them a little bit of your attention, as if you've got something else more important to do but you're so wonderful you manage to fit them in anyway and give them the benefit of your wonderfulness—'

'What the hell are you talking about, Robert? Are you mad or something? This is just – I don't know *what* you're talking about. It's not *me* you're thinking about at all. I just don't recognize—'

'Well, bad luck, you'd better learn to. Probably no one's told you; they probably feel sorry for you for being so pathetic,' he spat.

Ginny felt as if she were going to break in half.

'I don't know why he took you in,' she said. 'I'll never know why. You're just poison. You've got nothing to do with me, you don't want anything to do with him, and you don't *know* him – God, you don't *know* the effort he's making because he feels responsible to you. OK, so you're not interested in the bloody boat, but you ought to *pretend* . . . You know what you are? You're—'

'I don't need you to tell me who I am! At least he married my mother!'

'And *left* her, and I'm not surprised, if she spent all her time cleaning and polishing. God, how stupid! You know what you are? I'm going to tell you even if you don't want to hear – you're *nothing*. You're negative. You're a blank space full of hate, that's all you are. You don't do *anything*. So really I don't care a *shit* what you say about me, because at the end of the day at least I . . . at least I . . . At least I'm *trying*, I'm not just negative—'

'How do you know what I do, what I don't do?' he flared at her. 'You just assume that no one else but you's got any talent for anything. You know what? You've got a total contempt for anyone who isn't like you, d'you know that?'

'*Contempt*? What are you *talking* about, for God's sake?'

'You. I'm telling you what you're like. Everything's got to be on your terms. You're the most arrogant person I've ever met. You never show the slightest interest—'

'Yeah, and what happens when I do? You remember when I tried to talk to you, when you first came? All you did was lose your temper. I tried to make conversation, and you just got angry. Turning on me like a bloody pit bull or something. How long is a person supposed to go on trying? Or maybe I'm supposed to know all about you by *telepathy*, is that it? You give out *waves* or something – we're all supposed to pick them up without you having to soil yourself by talking? You make me sick, Robert. You and your mother, you both . . .'

She stopped. They were only a yard or so apart, she with her fists clenched, he still straddling the hammock. His face was tight with misery, his eyes glittering, and the tension in his shoulders was making his whole body shake. Suddenly she found, to her consternation and embarrassment, that her eyes were full of tears and that all the fury that had welled up from nowhere had drained away.

'This is stupid,' she muttered.

'You started it.'

'You did, actually. If you hadn't . . .'

The words ran out. She shrugged.

He looked down, ran his fingers through his hair. Then he wiped his eyes with the back of his hand.

'I don't understand you,' she said.

'Nothing to understand. You said it.'

'Yeah, but I didn't mean that. I meant . . . Oh, I just meant . . .' She sighed, terribly weary suddenly, and speaking the next words with a great effort: 'I just meant I can't understand you. Because . . . I don't *know* anything about you or your mother; I didn't even know you existed. It's no good asking Dad. If he's kept you secret from me all this time, and me from you . . . well, I can't trust him any more. Can't you see?'

He was still looking down. He bit savagely at a thumbnail and spat it out.

'She didn't tell me, either,' he said. 'I don't know any more than you do. I don't reckon there's any point in talking. It's a waste of breath. We've got nothing in common, we never will have. I'm not sure I want anything in common with you anyway.'

He swung his leg over the hammock and walked away. She watched him go, stifling the words that came to mind, words of appeal. She hadn't meant this to happen, she thought, but then she shook her head angrily at her own dishonesty: she'd meant something to happen, hadn't she? She'd wanted a fight, and she'd got one, and been hurt. Tough. Put up with it.

She brooded all the rest of the day over what he'd said, worrying at it like a dog for the scraps of truth that clung to it; because it couldn't all be true, she thought, surely. The idea of herself as a smug, patronizing snob was too painful to be borne. And it didn't *matter* that the house wasn't brilliantly clean, did it? Only to people with tiny minds who thought housework was important; or was that an example of her snobbery?

She was horribly confused and horribly unhappy, and the only thing that made it slightly better than it might have been was the realization that both she and Robert had held back from the final words that would have meant death, war, destruction, eternal hatred. The fact that she was black and he was white had no bearing on what they'd been quarrelling about, but it might have come up, and it hadn't.

As she went to bed she found another disagreeable feeling slink in and join all the others, and that was fear. If the *loa* – the gods of voodoo – could come so abruptly and fiercely as Baron Samedi had done the night before, what was to stop them from coming again? Had she opened some channel for them to use whenever they felt like it? What had she done? Was she entirely crazy?

Early next morning, just after Dad had gone to work, Ginny was in the kitchen fixing breakfast when the phone rang. She jumped with fright. Eventually, reluctantly, she picked it up.

'Hello?'

'Ginny. Hello. It's Wendy Stevens. Are you alone? Can we talk?'

'Yeah . . . Yeah! Fine! Dad's at work, and . . . Yeah.'

'How's Robert?'

Ginny paused. Robert was still in bed; they hadn't spoken since the quarrel. 'All right,' she said.

'I see. Well, listen, I've got some news for you. I'm not sure if I should be doing this – actually, I am sure, and I shouldn't. Did you know you'd been fostered?'

'What? Fostered? When? D'you mean I'm not – d'you mean that Dad's—'

'No, no, you're not fostered now. It was a long time ago – twelve, fourteen years or so. You don't remember?'

'No! God, no!'

'Well, never mind. You might remember, and that's my excuse. You know you told me about a caravan? And a woman called Maeve? And some woods where someone had been murdered?'

'Yes . . . go on . . .'

'Well, that reminded me of something, and I looked it up. There's a place not far from here called Staunton Chase, a wild sort of wood, and there was a big murder hunt there, oh, fifteen years ago. I thought it might have been there. So I asked a friend who works in the Social Services Department there. He's been there for a long time, knows everyone . . . Anyway, I told him about Maeve, and he recognized her at once. Her name's Mrs Sullivan. Apparently she does a lot of short-term fostering, especially for a Catholic home in the area; she's done it for years. He gave me her phone number, and I rang her up.'

'And . . . what did she say?'

'Well, she must've looked after hundreds of kids over the years. She didn't remember you at first, but then it came back. She said you were a difficult child.'

'Me? Why?'

'She said you used to scribble over everything. And there was something about make-up; I couldn't understand it . . .'

'I know what she means! I found it in the trailer and . . . But where was Dad? Why was I being fostered in the first place?'

'She didn't remember. She might not have known. There'd be no reason for her to.'

'Fostered . . . I don't believe it. Well, I do believe it, but why hasn't he told me?'

'I don't know, love. There's no way you're going to find out unless you ask him.'

Ginny said nothing. There was another way, and she'd just thought of it, but she didn't want to tell Wendy.

'Well,' she said. 'Thanks.'

'You've got my number if you want to get in touch?'

'Yeah. You gave me a card.'

'OK, then. I'll keep looking, see if I can find out anything else. But you're going to have to talk to him in the end.'

Ginny put the phone down, and hesitated, and then ran up to bang on Robert's door.

'What?' His voice was angry, wide awake.

She opened the door. He was lying fully clothed on the bed, hands behind his head.

'D'you want to find out the truth?' she demanded.

'The truth about what?'

'Us, of course. What you were saying yesterday. D'you want to find out or not?'

He sat up. 'How?'

'We've got to go *now* if you do. There's a train in ten minutes. You coming or not?'

'Where?'

'Chester.'

He shrugged. He was watching her carefully. 'All right.'

'Hurry, then. See you downstairs.'

She ran to her room, grabbed her rucksack, shoved a few things in it, stuffed the jacket on top, and took all the money she'd earned. She scribbled a note: *Gone out with Robert – back sometime*, and left it on the kitchen table; then she locked the back door and ran to the front, where Robert was waiting.

He looked at her rucksack. 'How long is this going to take?'

'As long as it takes. Come *on* – there's no time to hang about.'

*

At Porthafon they ran to the bus station, where there was a departure for Liverpool and Chester at eleven o'clock. They caught the bus with a minute to spare. Ginny, who had been shaking with nerves as they ran through the town in case she saw Joe Chicago, found herself relaxing as the bus pulled out and began to climb into the hills. She and Robert hadn't spoken on the train, but now they had three and a half hours to get through before the bus stopped in Chester. Ginny was sitting next to the window on the left, with her rucksack on the empty seat beside her, Robert across the aisle on the right. She was glad they weren't forced to sit any closer.

'What's in Chester, then?' he said finally.

'Dad's parents. Our grandparents.'

He frowned, puzzled.

'They'll know what happened, won't they?' she said impatiently. 'They know about me anyway, because I stayed with them once when I was a tiny kid. God knows why. But they'll know all about your mum and everything; they're bound to. So we'll go and ask them.'

'He's never mentioned them,' he said.

'No; he doesn't talk about them. There's too bloody much he doesn't talk about, and I'm sick of it. I just heard this morning . . . that phone call was Wendy Stevens, the social worker. She told me that

I'd been fostered when I was younger. I never knew. I mean, I don't mind or anything, but I ought to bloody know, I reckon.'

She was watching him closely, and she saw an honest bewilderment slowly growing. *All right*, she thought. *I don't like him, I'll never like him, but we're both in the same boat, Dad's messed us both up.*

And, briefly, a flicker of understanding passed between them, and what they understood was that this journey was a time out of battle, a time of truce.

She hesitated, and moved the rucksack on to her lap. He hesitated, and moved across to sit next to her. She began to tell him everything: Maeve and the trailer, Helen's first query about whether their father had been in prison, *Modern Painters* and the exhibition of her mother's paintings, Joe Chicago's jacket, Wendy's phone call.

At the end of it she said, 'Whatever it is he's done, I don't care, I can forgive him for it, but I can't forgive him for not telling me. Telling us.'

'This prison business,' he said. 'I can't believe it. You don't think it's got something to do with the murder in the woods – what's it called – Staunton Chase? You don't think he . . .'

'Course I've thought that. Of course I have. He's not a violent person, but who knows, Joe Chicago is, and if they knew each other and he got mixed up in something . . . I just don't know.'

'You think these grandparents will know who we are?'

'Course they will. You'll see.'

'They might not want to tell us anything, though.'

'They will. They'll have to.'

A long, hot journey, and then they had to buy a street map from a newsagent's in order to look up their way to Grove Road. They found a bus that took them to the nearest shop, next to a row of shops in neat 1930s brick, a wool shop and a florist's and a dress shop, all looking as if nothing had changed for fifty years. Grove Road, leading off the row of shops, was just as well preserved. Semi-detached houses, tidy gardens, net curtains; and stillness, on that blazing afternoon, without even the sound of sprinklers on lawns now that water was scarce, the very insects stunned into silence by the heat.

Number 16 was as obsessively neat and trim as all the rest. Two rosebushes stood inside the white-painted fence, and the paving stones that surrounded them had been swept and dusted. Ginny found herself thinking: *I remember those rosebushes*, but she knew she didn't; she could remember very little. She looked at Robert, whose eyes were screwed up against the glare off the road.

'Ready?' she said.

'They can only tell us to get lost,' he said. 'They can't kill us or anything . . .'

It sounded as if he was reassuring himself rather than her.

'That's right,' she said, and went up the little path and rang the bell.

Footsteps, a shadow behind the opaque glass; they caught each other's eye and exchanged a faint smile. Then their grandmother opened the door.

Chapter Thirteen
Golden years

She was in her sixties, stooped, grey-haired, with a closed, unhappy expression. She frowned at the two of them suspiciously.

'Mrs Howard?' Ginny said.

The woman nodded. 'Yes?' she said.

'Er . . . could we come in for a minute? It's a bit hard to explain . . .'

She looked over her shoulder doubtfully. 'Well, what's it about?' she said, looking at Robert with no more friendliness than she'd shown Ginny.

'It's a family matter,' he said.

Then her eyes flicked back to Ginny, and slowly at first and then suddenly, the realization flooded through her, changing her expression like a blush. One second she was closed up and dour, the next alert, and animated, and frightened.

'It's Virginia,' she whispered.

Ginny nodded. Her grandmother was holding the door tight as if to stop herself from falling. She looked at Robert again, and Ginny said, 'And my brother. Robert.'

'Janet's boy?'

'Yes,' he said. 'Can we come in?'

She looked overwhelmed, unable to move. There was a sound from behind her, and they looked past, down the hall and through the kitchen, and saw a man standing there, looking at them from outside the back door.

'Who is it?' he called.

'It's . . .' she began, then hastened back to speak to him from the kitchen door. 'It's Virginia! And Janet's boy!'

'Shut the door, then,' they heard him say urgently, as if the most important thing was to keep the neighbours from seeing. Ginny looked at Robert: did that mean they were going to be asked in, or not?

But their grandmother was back almost at once and urging them in. She shut the door hastily behind them. In the kitchen, their grandfather was standing on a sheet of newspaper and taking off his shoes before putting slippers on.

'Have you come from . . . ? Where's . . . ? Is your father . . . ?' She was nearly whispering in her confusion and emotion.

'No; he's at home,' Ginny said, finding her own voice weaker than she'd expected. 'He doesn't know we're here.'

'And Janet . . . My God, I don't know what to say. Is she . . . ?'

'She's dead,' said Robert. 'She died last month.'

'Oh, my dear . . . Ken? Did you hear? Janet's . . .'

He'd arrived in the hall by then, a heavy, quiet-looking man, with something of Dad's good looks but with a constant gnawing weakness about the mouth. Like his wife, he was utterly bewildered, quite unable to decide how to behave, what was the appropriate social form to adopt. Ginny felt that any naturalness had withered and died in them long before, and that if there was no established ritual to follow, they were lost, like children.

'Shall we—' she said, and he said simultaneously, 'Why don't we—' and she was opening the door of the front room, and Ginny and Robert went through.

Now Ginny began to remember things. The smell: wax polish, potpourri; the little carriage clock on the mantelpiece; the faded pink of the loose covers on the furniture. There was one picture on the wall – a woodland scene in a pretentious gilt frame, of the sort sold by the thousand in the furniture departments of large stores. No other pictures, no books, no records; just a hideous china cart-horse with leather reins standing on the windowsill, and the TV set in the corner, with a lace doily on top of it and a little brass pot of artificial flowers.

She looked around, Robert close beside her, and heard whispering outside the door. A moment later their grandfather came in.

'Well . . . Sit down, sit down,' he said. 'Make yourselves at home, come on . . . How old are you now, Virginia? Eh?'

'Sixteen,' she said, sitting on the sofa. Robert sat next to her.

'And you . . . er . . .'

'Robert. I'm sixteen too.'

'Ah. Yes . . . Getting on all right at school?'

She nodded. He shrugged. 'All right, I suppose,' he said.

'Good. That's the style.'

He sat down heavily in the armchair by the fireplace.

'Have you had some tea?' he said.

'No,' said Ginny. 'We came straight here from the bus station.'

'Grandma's getting some now. Soon be ready. Have you . . . come a long way?'

'Yeah. From home.'

'And . . . where's . . . ?'

'You don't know where we live?'

He shook his head.

'Llangynog,' Robert said. 'In Wales.'

'Oh, Wales? And your father, has he . . . he's not coming with you?'

'He doesn't know we're here. This was our idea,' said Ginny, looking at Robert. 'We thought we'd just like to find out about things. We didn't tell him. So . . . I found out your address and we just came. That's it, really.'

'Ah. Yes. Right. Well, it's a big surprise, naturally; we're not prepared or anything . . . You're a big girl now, Virginia; I'd never have recognized you. And your mother? How's she getting on these days?'

He wouldn't look either of them in the eye, or if he did, he'd look away after a second and direct his gaze over their shoulders or above their heads, so it wasn't clear who this last question was directed at. Ginny and Robert looked at each other, and then Robert looked back at him and said, 'Mum's dead. She died a short while ago. That's why I'm living with Dad and Ginny, you see.'

'Oh! I'm sorry. I didn't grasp what she was saying out there, what she was going to say . . . My dear boy, I . . . I'm very sorry to hear about that. She'd been ill, had she? Or . . . ?'

'Yes,' Robert said. 'She'd been ill for a few months.'

'Ah,' he said. 'And what about your grandmother?

Kitty? I heard that Janet's father had, er, passed away a few years back, but . . .'

'She lives in Spain now,' Robert said. 'She married someone with a lot of money. She sort of lost touch with us, I think.'

Hearing him talk like this was a revelation to Ginny, and to hear him refer to her by name and call her Ginny and not Virginia, as their grandparents were doing, made it almost worth coming all this way.

'What should we call you?' she said into the little silence.

'Oh, I should think it would have to be Grandad, don't you? And Grandma.'

'Because, you see, there're a lot of things we don't know. And we really came here to see if you could tell us . . .' Ginny trailed off as the door opened.

'I expect you'd like to wash your hands,' said their grandmother. 'D'you remember where it is, Virginia?'

'No. Sorry. I was only four or something . . .'

'Oh, less than that, I think,' said Grandma, showing her the way.

Well, Robert should like this house, Ginny thought in the bathroom. Every corner of it was obsessively clean, the windows sparkled, the water in the lavatory was blue and foaming, two neatly folded towels hung side by side on the rack. Despite the cleanliness, there was a closed-up, unused feeling in the air, as if no one had visited the house for years, no one had trodden the carpets or drawn the curtains or looked out of the windows but that silent, awkward, broken couple downstairs. And everything was so *ugly*. Didn't they have any idea how ugly it was? Or was that just her snobbery again?

She passed Robert on the stairs, and he blew out his cheeks and rolled his eyes, obviously finding it as difficult as she was.

Grandma was standing by another door, which Ginny vaguely remembered led into the dining room. The layout of the house was coming back to her, but it all seemed so small, so cramped. Grandma smiled, and Ginny smiled back, nervous formal smiles both of them, and then to her surprise her grandmother gave her a brief tight hug and then stepped away quickly. Ginny had no time to respond.

In the few minutes since they'd arrived, Grandma had laid the dining room table with a tablecloth, a silver teapot, cups and saucers, a plate of bread and butter, a cake, biscuits . . . It was as if it had been ready and waiting for years.

Ginny, fighting her shyness, said, 'I can hardly remember what it was like, being here before.'

'Well, you weren't here for long; just a few days. And then your daddy came and took you away, and . . . that was that,' she said with an attempt at brightness. 'How is he? Is he all right?'

'Yeah, he's fine. He's – you know – working and things. He bought a boat last week. We haven't actually been out in it yet.'

'Oh, a boat, eh?' said Grandad, who'd come in quietly.

'Is he . . . did he ever marry again?' said Grandma.

'Oh, no. No. See, he was never divorced from Robert's mum,' Ginny said.

They both nodded wisely, as if they'd expected something of the sort, but Ginny could tell they were surprised.

Grandad turned to the door. 'Here's the boy,' he said, with a fragile heartiness. 'Come and sit down. We'll have some tea, eh?'

'Expect you're hungry,' said Grandma as they all sat down. 'Come a long way.'

'How did you get here?' said Grandad. 'On the train?'

'No. There aren't any trains. On a bus,' Ginny said.

'Oh, so you said, yes, the bus station . . .'

Polite, empty words, formal teatime courtesy: have a biscuit, let me cut you some cake, would you like some more tea. It seemed to go on for ever. Ginny knew that Robert felt as she did, that he wanted to bang the table and shake their stupid old tortoise heads and shout, *Tell us the truth, for God's sake!* And, like her, he was reining it in for Dad's sake – being polite to Dad's parents out of consideration for him.

Finally she'd had enough.

'Look, *please*,' she said, 'we want to ask you about Dad and everything, that's why we've come. Because Robert and I, we don't know anything about the family . . . I mean, I didn't know anything about Robert till a few weeks ago, I'd never heard of him, even, and I thought my mother was married to Dad. I never dreamed any of it would be like it is, and then I remembered being here when I was little, and I thought you'd probably know . . .'

Her voice trailed off. They were sitting like sculptures: Robert looking down at his plate, Grandad gazing fixedly at the wall, Grandma with her eyes closed altogether. It was as if they'd all lost the use of sight but Ginny, and she was looking from one to the other, her eyes doing the asking that her voice had given up, and feeling herself hot-cheeked with embarrassment. Why did they have to behave like this? Was she different again, inwardly as well as visibly?

But then Robert helped her.

He looked up and said, 'Yeah. That's right. See, Mum – my mother – she never told me anything. About you or about Dad. Nothing. It was just as if you – he'd – never existed. And I didn't know about Ginny, either. So I never knew Dad, and I don't know him now, really, not to ask about things. And Ginny can't ask him because he never told her about me, so we're both in the dark.'

'And you're the only people we can ask,' Ginny added. 'That's why we came. We won't tell him about it, if you don't want us to.'

After a moment their grandmother said, 'Is he treating you all right?'

Grandad shifted as if he was uncomfortable. Ginny nodded. Robert said, 'Yeah. He's very . . . kind. But we just want to know where we come from.'

That was so exactly what Ginny wanted that she could only look at him and nod eagerly. Then Grandad put both hands on the table and stood up.

'Let's go in the front room,' he said. 'We'll be more comfortable in there. Can't talk comfortably at the tea table . . .'

*

It had begun just after the war. Grandad had a great friend, Arthur Weaver, and when they left the army, they set up a little business together, selling motor parts, and then within a month of each other they both got married. Grandad and Grandma – Ken and Dorothy – and Arthur and Kitty became inseparable. They went to the cinema together; they took turns giving each other dinner every weekend after which they'd play bridge; they shared holidays; borrowed each other's lawnmowers and power drills and slide projectors; even took up the same hobbies – golf, camping, wine-making. When Tony was born to Dorothy, and Janet six months later to Kitty, it seemed as if some kind of seal had been set on this wonderful friendship. It was a golden time, Grandad said, and Grandma said separately that they were golden years . . .

Ginny listened to this recital with powerful curiosity. This was where she came from – half of her: this narrow, prim, cosy, insufferably complacent world of bridge parties and polishing the car and pruning the roses and unfailingly voting Conservative. It was like another planet. But nothing was more alien to her than that friendship, the obsessive repetition of Arthur and Kitty, Arthur and Kitty, Arthur and Kitty. It was more than a friendship; it was more like a four-way marriage, and Ginny, used to the casual independent freedom she shared with Dad, felt oppressed and claustrophobic as she thought about it. It wasn't natural; it was asking for trouble.

Clearly, though, it had been the biggest thing in Grandad's life, at least Ginny wasn't so sure about her grandmother; there was something hooded, shadowed, about her manner as she nodded and echoed his words, as if for her there'd been a question at the heart of it all. But she joined in as he got out some photograph albums, with dozens upon dozens of pictures carefully dated and labelled: Arthur and Kitty at Blackpool, Dad as a little boy with a tricycle, Dad in school uniform, Grandad and Arthur playing golf, Dad and Janet . . .

Robert was gazing at the pictures of his mother, his eyes fierce, as if he wanted to drag her back to life. To Ginny's mind she looked wilful: dark and pretty and strong-minded, with a tight set to her lips.

'And as time went by,' Grandad was saying, 'well, we all assumed it would just be the natural thing if the two of them, in the fullness of time, if they were to marry . . .'

'We never pushed them into it,' said Grandma.

'Oh, Lord, no. Absolutely not. It was always

understood that they were free to do as they pleased, no pressure on them at all, free agents.'

'I know Arthur and Kitty both wanted it, though,' she said. 'They said so more than once.'

'Well, so did we,' he said. 'No point in denying it.'

They were silent for a moment. Then Grandad opened another photograph album.

'Here we are,' he said. 'The wedding.'

'Oh, it was such a happy day,' said Grandma. 'Everything about it seemed to be blessed, somehow.'

The formal clothes, a young Dad with his hair long, Janet queenly and proud, screwing up her eyes against the sun . . .

'It's the bride's parents' place to lay on the wedding, of course,' said Grandad, 'but we'd gone shares in everything else, we couldn't hold back now. We gave them a wonderful wedding, honeymoon in Tenerife. Then . . . just a short while afterwards, it all seemed to go wrong.'

'Did Janet . . . did your mum ever talk about those days?' said Grandma delicately to Robert.

'No. Not a word. Honest, I've never heard any of this before. She was very . . . she kept herself to herself, I suppose. We never talked much about anything.'

'How did it go wrong?' Ginny asked Grandad.

'Well . . . we still don't know all the details. Because he didn't speak to us, you see. We knew something was going wrong. First thing we knew was Arthur . . .'

'He came to us one day,' said Grandma. 'Janet had gone home to him and Kitty with some terrible story Tony – your dad – had suddenly told her. Arthur was shaken. He was white, he was . . . We'd never seen him in a state like that.'

Grandad nodded. 'Naturally Janet wouldn't, she couldn't, well, she, she didn't want anything to do with him any more, didn't want to see him again, it was all over.'

'Broke our hearts,' she said.

'Arthur had to come and speak to us on her behalf. Painful. Terrible time.'

Ginny was lost. So, she saw, was Robert, who turned to her, frowning in puzzlement. She said, 'But why? I don't get it. Dad had gone to his wife, Robert's mum, and he'd told her some terrible story and she wouldn't speak to him any more? What was this terrible story? It wasn't the car crash, was it? The broken bridge?'

That was a helpless guess. They looked blank, and Grandma shook her head.

'Car crash?' said Grandad. 'I'm sorry, my dear, I

don't know what you mean. No, it was the old story: it was the other woman. It was your mother. We had no idea; we were knocked sideways by it. Came right out of the blue.'

'He wanted Janet to adopt . . .' Grandma began, but went no further.

'Yes, when your mother left you there with the nuns,' Grandad said, 'he wanted Janet to agree to—'

'What? *Left* me? Left me with the nuns? What nuns?'

'The nuns in the children's home.'

'But what d'you mean, *left* me there? I thought she died.'

'Well . . .' They looked at each other, alarmed at Ginny's tone.

Then Grandad said, 'If that's what he told you, then I'm sure that's . . . You see, we weren't in any position to know; we had it all via Arthur. Tony wanted Janet to agree to adopt you, you see, make it look decent, you know, put a decent face on it, but she said no. Wouldn't budge, wouldn't buy it. Not at any price. So there they were. Breaking up over a thing like that. Not that Tony told us. It all came via Arthur. He – Arthur, I mean – he was very bitter, very cut up about it.'

Breaking up over a thing like that, Ginny thought.

So I'm a thing like that. Nice to know at last. A thing like that.

'Of course, it was the end for the firm,' Grandad went on. 'Put the skids under the partnership. Thirty years of friendship, lying in ruins . . . Arthur bought out my share of the firm, and shortly after that he sold the whole shoot, the whole boiling. Made a tidy sum. I don't know, I'm not bitter exactly, but . . . We'd see them sometimes, Arthur and Kitty. They'd just pass by without a word. Not the slightest flicker. It was as if those thirty years had never happened. Just been a dream.'

That seemed to be the end, as far as they were concerned. They sat looking down at the floor in the furniture-polished silence.

'But . . . what happened then?' said Ginny. 'I mean, what about me – what did Dad do? And these nuns – how long was I with them?'

The old couple looked at each other. It was a complicated look: there was a sort of furtive anxiety in it, and guilt, and even a sly I-told-you-so triumph – but which feeling came from which partner, Ginny couldn't have said.

'We don't rightly know,' said Grandad. 'Tony, your dad, well, he just took off. Left his wife and . . .' He looked at Robert, and then away again; his eyes never rested on anyone for long. 'Well, we thought, naturally, he'd gone off with his fancy woman. Your mother. Left you in the children's home, done a runner. There was no sign, no word from him, nothing.'

'But she was dead!' Ginny said again. 'And he wouldn't have just *left* me there! It's not like him. I mean, I *know* him, after all. He's not like that . . .'

But I was fostered, she found herself thinking. *He must have left me sometime. And why do they keep talking about Maman as if she was alive? They're not telling me the truth. I don't believe them. They're all liars in this family.*

'What about when Ginny stayed here?' asked Robert, coming to her aid.

'Yes,' she said. 'Did the nuns bring me here? Or what? I thought it was him, but I can't remember.'

Then a strange thing began to happen. Ginny sensed it, and she knew that Robert did too: a change in the atmosphere as instant and definite as if a spotlight had been switched on. She wouldn't have been surprised if there'd been an audible click.

The effect was that her grandmother had suddenly become the focus of the room, like a surprise witness in a murder trial. She hadn't said a word or moved a muscle, but something invisible, some emotional charge – guilt, anger – had leapt to her like a spark crossing a gap and changed her personality. It was a different woman looking out of her eyes, and Ginny quailed.

'That was cruel,' said Grandma in a new, louder voice.

Ginny thought: *What? What I said was cruel? Or something else?* Her scalp crawled with a sort of sickening embarrassment.

But Grandma was going on: 'We were doing our best. It wasn't much to offer. God knows, it was all we had, but apparently it wasn't enough . . .'

Ginny was aware of her grandfather sitting up in his chair, his face full of fear. Something bad was in the air.

'But what about my mother?' she said shakily.

The old woman sat up. Her eyes were bright with violence. 'Yes,' she said, 'I'll tell you about her . . .'

'Dorothy,' murmured Grandad.

She turned on him, those eyes full of danger. 'Yes, Ken? I was under the impression that Virginia had asked me a question.'

He shrank back from the blaze of hatred, nodding, saying, 'Yes, dear, yes . . .'

'I'm allowed to speak, am I?'

'Of course . . . yes . . .'

Ginny thought: *He's used to this – he's seen her go crazy before – he knew it was coming – and now she's going to turn to me . . .*

She did, and Ginny felt a chill at the roots of her soul as those bright eyes found hers. Without knowing how it had happened, she was holding Robert's hand among the sofa cushions, and they clung together like children as Grandma said:

'So I can answer Virginia's question? Well, I'm sorry, dear, but it's got to be said, it's wrong not to tell you, I can't let you live with a stain on your past. It's not a nice word, but I can't help it: your mother is a whore. A black whore. You know what I—'

'A *what*?' Ginny said. 'And what d'you mean, *is*?' She thought she wasn't hearing properly. This was impossible, surely.

'Dorothy, please,' Grandad whispered.

'Don't you dare interrupt me!' she flared at him. 'If you'd had the guts to deal with it at the time, everything would have been all right, but no, leave it to Dorothy, leave it all to Dorothy, that's your motto. Yes, Virginia, God knows it's not your fault, dear, but to think of my boy, my son, my only child, wallowing in coloured filth when he had a decent home, a pretty wife, the best background a man could have . . . Well, he'd never have done it if she hadn't tempted him. Stands to reason. She knew a good thing when she saw one, and she grabbed it with both hands. That's her type. If the only way to climb out of the gutter was to steal another woman's husband, then she wouldn't let decency stand in the way . . .'

The stream of venom continued to pour out, even when Ginny had stood up, even after she'd begun to speak, her shaking voice trying to drown her grandmother's: 'Thank you for the tea. It was very nice. I'm sorry I seem to be the wrong colour. It must be my mother's fault, like everything else. Spoiling your wonderful golden dream, yes, it must've been horrible for you, but never mind, that's it, I'm going now. Goodbye.'

Her grandmother's voice trailed off.

Grandad was trying to get up, but Ginny brushed past him and seized her rucksack from the hall floor. She was fumbling with the front door handle when she heard her grandmother behind her and turned in fury – but the old woman was holding her arms out, just an old woman again, her face blind with tears.

'Virginia – darling – listen: You've always been my dear little grandchild – my first one. If I said anything wrong, I'm sorry, I'm so sorry, I didn't want to offend you. I'm a stupid old woman – stupid. You're my little granddaughter, I love you, I want you to be happy. Is he mistreating you? Is he looking after you? A man can't do it on his own. She shouldn't have left him, it wasn't fair, it wasn't right. My darling, I only want what's best for you . . .'

And Ginny let herself be hugged and kissed, controlling her disgust at the wetness of tears on her cheek, the smell of stale face powder, the bony looseness of the old woman's body against hers. She stood it for a few seconds and then twisted away. The whole thing was horrible.

'Is she alive?' she demanded. 'Is my mother alive?'

'Oh, darling – forget all about her—'

'She is, isn't she? Or are you making it up?'

'Darling, don't say that – stay with us – we'll look after you – she won't want you now—'

Ginny twisted aside and ran out of the door and off down the road, trying not to be sick.

There was a bus coming; without waiting for Robert, she waved it to a halt, bought a ticket to the town centre, sat down trembling.

Black whore.

Wallowing in coloured filth.

There'd been so many blows, from so many different directions, raining in so suddenly, that Ginny was dazed; and the hardest blow of all was the suggestion that her mother was alive. It was impossible, ridiculous. She dragged *Modern Painters* out of her rucksack and looked again at the advertisement:

it merely said *Haitian Painting of the Past Twenty Years*, which didn't help at all.

Seeing a railway station, she jumped up impulsively and rang the bell to stop the bus. She felt a faint anxiety about Robert. She'd dragged him all this way; shouldn't she go back and . . .

No. He could find the bus station by himself, surely; for the moment, this was more urgent.

At a phone booth in the station, she dialled the number of the art gallery. There was no answer for a long time, and she began to beat her fist softly against her head.

'Hello. L'Ouverture Gallery.'

It was a soft Scottish voice. Ginny, startled by an answer at last, nearly dropped the magazine.

'Oh. Hello. I'm ringing about your exhibition – the paintings from Haiti—'

'Yes. It's opening tomorrow.'

'Er . . . one of the painters, Anielle Baptiste . . .'

'Yes?'

'Could you tell me about her work, what you've got there? I mean, I'm a student, you see, and I've seen some of her work before, but only in reproduction. And I'm not here for long . . .'

'Oh, right. Well, there's a number of paintings from her election series; they haven't been shown here before.'

'Election series?'

'She did some pictures based on the Haitian general election. And there's a quite extraordinary painting called *The Death of Colonel Paul*. It's well worth a visit for that one alone. And some landscapes.'

'What election was that?'

'The one they had recently, when it all ended in violence. Two years ago, three maybe. I ought to know—'

'Sorry, when did you say? Two years ago?'

A puzzled laugh. 'Yes, that's right. You said you're not in Liverpool for long?'

Ginny was breathless. 'Not long, no.'

'And you're a student? Well, why don't you come along tonight? We're having a private view, but we're not fussy; it's not formal or anything. Come and join the party. The more the merrier. What's your name?'

'Oh, thanks . . . Ginny Howard. Who would I say told me to come?'

'I'm the owner, Paul Chalmers. I won't forget. You might meet the artist herself. She's coming along later. See you at about seven, then.'

Ginny blindly put the phone down. All the golden years had come to this, and there was no going back now.

Chapter Fourteen
The Death of Colonel Paul

The L'Ouverture Gallery was situated in a street not far from the docks. Ginny had managed to buy a Liverpool street map at the railway station in Chester before the train left, and she spent the journey alternately poring over it and gazing unseeingly out of the train window, smiling from time to time with something that felt absurdly like happiness. The walk from Lime Street Station to the street where the gallery was took twenty minutes. Of Liverpool itself she registered nothing.

She got there at five to seven and made herself stop and look at things in order to calm down. The narrow street seemed to have had three lives, and it still bore traces of each of them: the first as a sternly prosperous area of offices for shipping firms and cotton merchants; the second as a seedy, downmarket collection of flyblown newsagents and dusty tailors' shops; and now its third life was beginning, based on nebulous trendy things like design and lifestyle, with a very expensive clothes shop, an architectural practice, a wine bar, and the L'Ouverture Gallery.

The gallery was a wide glass-fronted place with a display of sculptures in the window. There were paintings on the oatmeal-coloured wall, but Ginny couldn't see them clearly from across the street; and there was someone moving about inside.

She crossed the street. Her heart was hammering so hard she thought they must be able to hear it in the wine bar. She looked at a poster on the gallery door advertising the exhibition, and then knocked on the glass. The man inside looked up and waved.

He was in his thirties, plump, wearing the kind of clothes they sold in the expensive shop next door. And he was black, and the moment he spoke, she realized that his was the Scottish voice from the telephone, and she felt surprise, and shame at the white part of her that could be surprised, and a simple curiosity as to whether she herself sounded Welsh.

'You're Ginny Howard,' he said.

'And you're Mr Chalmers? Thanks; this is really nice of you. I can't tell you—'

'That's OK. I was a student once. Come in. You could give me a hand, if you liked.'

He was preparing a buffet, or rather peeling the

cling-film from one that had been prepared earlier: dishes of salad, plates of cold pizza, fried chicken, and various bits and pieces she supposed were Caribbean. He asked Ginny to take some wineglasses out of a cardboard box and set them on the table, and then to put some paper napkins in between the plates stacked at one end, and altogether it felt like being back at the Yacht Club. She realized guiltily that Angie Lime would have been expecting her, and she hadn't let them know. She realized, less guiltily, that Dad would be wondering where she and Robert were . . . No, all that was too complicated to think about. Push it out of sight.

Paul Chalmers was asking her a question. She gathered herself and said, 'No, my father's English, but my mother came from Haiti, which is why I'm interested in . . . And I saw some of Anielle Baptiste's work illustrated in an article, I can't remember, some American magazine, and I thought I really can't miss this, I've got to see it. It's really good of you to let me come . . .'

'She's the star of this exhibition, but we haven't made an issue of it; there's a lot of good work besides hers. We've hung her pictures in the large room, through there. Do you want to put your rucksack in the office? Through the door and on the left.'

There was a narrow corridor with some unframed pictures in a wooden stand against the wall. It was carpeted in neat oatmeal like the rest of the gallery, and it all looked new and clean. She put her rucksack in the little office, and then, noticing that there was a lavatory next door, gave in to the feeling that had been plucking at her stomach and went in to be sick. She crouched there shivering as if she had the flu, wishing she'd never come, wishing Robert's mother were still alive so that she would never have heard of him, never have disturbed this whole horrible tangle.

But it was no good. Here she was, and in an hour or so she'd meet her mother. She stood up, ran some water, washed, and went back to the gallery.

Paul Chalmers was talking on the phone, so she walked through to the large room, where her mother's paintings were hung.

When Ginny was first becoming interested in art and the history of painting, Dad had given her a big book with hundreds of reproductions in it. She'd pored over it with more than delight – with a kind of greed, in fact. She absorbed everything the book told her about the Renaissance, and the Impressionists, and the Cubists, about Botticelli and Monet and Picasso, and she breathed it all in like oxygen she hadn't known she was missing. And among the pictures in the book, there were two that made her gasp. One was Whistler's *Arrangement in Grey and Black*, his portrait of his mother sitting on an upright chair, and the other was El Greco's *View of Toledo*. She remembered her reaction quite clearly: a sudden intake of breath, caused by sheer surprise at the arrangement of shapes and colours. It was a physical shock.

And when she looked at the big painting that dominated the end wall, the same thing happened. It would have affected her the same way whoever had painted it, because it was a masterpiece. What it showed was a middleaged black man, in a gaudy uniform with epaulettes and medals, in the act of falling on to the red-carpeted floor of a lushly furnished room. He'd been eating a meal, and on the table beside him was a plate of yellow soup. Beyond him, through the open door and at the open window, stood a crowd of people, watching: white people and black, old and young, richly dressed and poverty-stricken. Some of them carried objects that helped you understand who they were: a wad of dollar bills for a banker, a syringe for a drug addict, a clutch of guns for an arms dealer, a chicken for a peasant; and the expressions on their faces told Ginny that they'd all in some ways been victims or accomplices of the man who was dying.

And all that was important, but just as important was the strange discord the particular red of the carpet set up with the particular yellow of the soup, so that you knew it was something significant, and you guessed the soup had been poisoned. And the way the dying man was isolated by that acid red from every other shape in the picture, so that it looked as if he were sinking out of sight in a pool of blood. And mainly what was important was the thing that was impossible to put into words: the arrangement of the shapes on the canvas. These same elements put together differently would have been an interesting picture, but put together like this, they made Ginny catch her breath and put out a hand to the wall.

'Tell me why it's good,' said the voice of Paul Chalmers behind her.

She tried to say what was in her mind and how it had affected her. She tried to say that here was a way of painting that was true to everything she knew: to the European fine art tradition, and to the storytelling part of her too, and it was about blackness, about a black society and its experience of itself.

He listened seriously and nodded.

'D'you think a black person paints differently

from a white person, then?' he asked when she'd finished.

It was her own question, coming back at her. But in front of these paintings, at last, she thought she could see the beginnings of an answer.

'Not . . . not in the way they'd put paint on the canvas. No. Or in the way they *saw*, even. The rules of perspective would be the same. But . . . but the point is that we never see a picture just as itself. Maybe we should; I don't know. But what we feel and think when we look at a picture is . . . well, it's part of how we see it, isn't it? We look at it with everything we already know. And we can't ignore that, because it's part of us.'

'Go on,' he said.

'Well, when I saw this, I thought of Whistler, straight away. The *Arrangement in Grey and Black*, you know? And so that's part of my experience of this painting. The fact that it's part of a European tradition. She speaks the same language. But at the same time . . . You see that mark up there? The man's drawing it in chalk on the wall?'

'What is it?'

'It's the *vever* of Erzulie.'

She looked at him, but he didn't know what she meant. She explained, and then said, 'And that's important too. Because I don't know what this man

241

Colonel Paul had done, but one of the things that's going to survive him is . . . love. I think that's what it means. But it's also there like a secret symbol for those people who know what it is. And knowing that it's to do with voodoo . . .' She struggled to find her way back to what she'd started to say. 'Well, I can't block out all those things I know and just think of the picture as shapes and colours. So I have to accept them and take in the picture with my mind as well as my eyes, and if my mind knows that the artist is black . . . then maybe there *is* a difference between black art and white art. I mean, if a black person points out that a black politician is corrupt, then at least you know they're not saying it out of racism. But if a white person says it . . . you couldn't be sure. Unless you knew them. I'm not being very clear . . .'

He was listening carefully, frowning.

'Where are you studying?'

'Oh . . .' She blushed. 'I'm still at school. I said I was a student, but . . . I'm a school student.'

'What do you want to do?'

'Go to art school and paint.'

'Why do you think Baptiste wanted to paint this? To say something about this guy, Colonel Paul?'

'Yes . . . But not mainly. What I think she mainly wanted to do was to see what happened when she put that red and that yellow together. That's what would have started it for me anyway. Some little technical thing like that. And the shape of the man as he falls . . . See, because there's no shadow, you can't sort of see easily where he is in relation to the floor. He seems to be floating in space, almost. But if you work it out by taking a fix on the table and the leg of the chair, you can see that she's got it right, it's technically correct – he hasn't got his foot through the plane of the carpet or anything. She just hasn't given us any clues. Doing that is fantastically difficult, and yet she's just done it without any fuss. It's just . . . Oh, God, I'm amazed. It's brilliant!'

She felt a lump in her throat and had to stop talking. She didn't feel in the least self-conscious with the man. He was part of her world, the world of art.

She looked around at the other paintings, swallowing hard so that she could speak again.

'These are the election pictures? God, what happened?'

'It all went wrong,' he said. 'After years of dictatorship, maybe it's hard to make a democracy work.'

The pictures were uncomfortable to look at: a man mutilated in the dust of a Haitian street, his blood half-dry in the hot sun; a dead child huddled in a doorway; a smiling man with dark glasses firing a machine gun into a crowded church. They were swiftly painted in crude colours, but under each of them Ginny could see that total technical assurance: the artist knew exactly how limbs fitted together, how shadows fell, how the perspective of a sloping street worked, so there was no hesitation between seeing and painting. Not a second of doubt. There was something pitiless there too. A ferocious unblinking stare, like that of a bird of prey.

There was one small landscape that wasn't in the election series, but it had the same fierce quality: sparse green fields bordering a sluggish yellow-brown river. From one side a narrow wooden bridge led out across the water, but it didn't reach the other side because it had collapsed halfway. Clumsy spars of wood trailed in the water.

'A broken bridge,' said Ginny to herself in wonder, and then there were other voices from the front of the gallery. The first guests were arriving.

She hurried back through to help. Soon she was pouring wine, hanging coats, offering catalogues as if she belonged there. What would it be like one day to have a show like this, to see her work hanging in a gallery, being admired and discussed and bought? Not as good as doing it, she thought. That was the best part. There was so much to learn.

And all the time she was thinking: *When's she going to come? What's she going to be like? Will she know me?*

At about eight o'clock there was a stir among the people by the door, and without any warning, there she was.

She was shorter than Ginny had expected, and her hair was speckled with grey, though her face was unlined. It was the face in Ginny's photograph, no question about it, but stronger, colder, more austere. She was smiling now, talking to Paul Chalmers and some guests, accepting a glass of wine, and although she was animated and friendly, no one would diminish her by a word like 'charming'; she was too powerful for that. She was dressed in what looked like a very expensive cream silk suit, and around her neck she wore a string of heavy bright beads. Her hair was cut short, like Ginny's. Did they look alike? Would anyone notice?

Trying not to stare, Ginny carried on attending to the guests, opening wine, disposing of dirty plates, making conversation. There were about forty people there, white and black, respectable-looking and artistic-looking, and they weren't hard to talk to; they seemed to accept that since she was there, she belonged there.

And at every moment she was aware of where

her mother was, of whom she was talking to, of where she was looking. When eventually her mother moved through to the larger room, Ginny followed, and presently she gathered her courage and spoke to her.

'Er . . . Miss Baptiste, can I ask you something? Why is the man up there, why is he drawing Erzulie's *vever* on the wall?'

'Oh, you know what that is? You know about voodoo?'

She spoke with an American accent, but the word 'voodoo' sounded like *vaudou*, as if it were French.

'Well, just a little. Only what someone told me. Am I right? Is that what it is?'

'Yes, that's what it is. But I don't know why he's doing it. It shouldn't be on a wall anyway; it's a sacred thing; it should be drawn in meal on the ground. I guess he doesn't know what he's doing any more than I do.'

'Who was Colonel Paul?'

'An army officer. The Americans wanted to extradite him to face drug charges, but he was popular with the army in Haiti. Someone poisoned him with a plate of pumpkin soup.'

'I think it's brilliant.'

'Thank you . . .'

She was turning away to the two people waiting

to talk on her other side. Ginny, desperate, said, 'Please . . . Could I show you something?'

She turned back. 'OK. What is it?'

'It's . . . Could you just come in the office a minute? It's in there . . .'

A slight shrug, an indifferent expression, but she followed Ginny through the door, into the neat cool oatmeal-clean corridor, into the office. Ginny fumbled open the rucksack with shaking hands. She was intensely conscious of the woman in the small room with her, of her expensive clothes, her American accent, her severe manner; they all made Ginny feel small and provincial and unimportant.

She found the photograph in its leather frame, her mother's picture, and held it out.

'What's—' said her mother, and then fell still. Her eyes glittered as she looked down at the photograph of her younger self. 'Where did you get this?' she went on harshly.

Ginny could hardly speak. 'It's . . . my mother. It's you. I've always had it.'

Her mother looked at her, briefly, and then back at the photograph before turning away.

'You're making a mistake,' she said.

'No! I'm not! Dad – my father – he always told me about you. I thought you were dead.'

But Anielle Baptiste was shaking her head.

'It has nothing to do with me. This is a mistake. I'm a painter, I'm not a mother. Excuse me, I have to go and see the guests—'

'Oh, *please* – it isn't a mistake – you *must* listen. I'm your *daughter*—'

Her mother was at the door. Ginny was still helplessly holding out the photograph.

'I don't know what you mean. All I can say is you've made a mistake.'

She was turning the handle, about to open the door. Ginny rushed forward the three or four steps between them, but stopped before touching her, held away by the formality, that severe, elegant force of character, those cold eyes.

'Just tell me – listen, I promise I won't bother you. I swear I'll go away right now and never see you again, you won't ever hear of me – but just *tell* me, for God's sake: is it true or not? Are you my mother?'

The woman looked away. Her hand on the doorknob, strong, square, with paint ineradicably staining the rims of her nails, was the only thing about her that didn't look glossy and fashionable. Ginny lowered her eyes and looked at that hand; it was the only place she thought she'd be able to make contact.

She reached out to touch it. Her mother let

Ginny's hand rest there but gave nothing back, neither moving to hold it nor taking her own away, and after a second or so Ginny dropped hers to her side.

'What's your name?' said her mother.

'Ginny. Howard.' It was a hoarse whisper through the lump in her throat.

'You're interested in painting?'

'It's the only thing—'

'It's not the only thing. It's not even the most important thing.'

'What . . .' Ginny still couldn't speak properly. 'What is the most important thing?'

There was a long, long silence.

Then Anielle Baptiste slowly turned away and opened the door.

She said, 'Painting isn't the most important thing, but it'll have to do till we find out what is.'

Ginny held out her hand again.

'Please! You haven't answered my question! You can't – you mustn't—'

But the woman was halfway out of the room, and then she'd left it entirely. Her back was turned. The soft neon strip light above her in the narrow corridor gave her figure the look of the dying Colonel Paul – weightless, without a fixed position, either floating or sinking but in any case out of human reach.

Without looking back, she opened the door to the gallery and went through.

Ginny was left in the office doorway. Holding herself with great care, like someone trying to avoid spilling a glass that was filled to the brim, she turned back inside, put the photograph into the rucksack, slung the jacket over her shoulders, and went out through a back entrance into a little yard, into the street beyond, into the city.

Chapter Fifteen

Arrangement in Pink and Yellow

Twenty-four hours later, Ginny got off the bus in Porthafon, and stiffly, reluctantly, made her way through the town to the row of council houses by Mr Alston's garden furniture factory, and stood by the gate of one of them.

Most of its neighbours had been sold to their tenants; they had stone cladding over the front, or new ranch-style porches, or fancy diamond-paned windows. This one didn't. The window frames were in need of painting, and the garden was a tangle of long grass and weeds. It was Joe Chicago's house, and Ginny was going to return the jacket.

She'd come to that decision in the early hours of the morning, on a bench near the station in Liverpool, at the moment when the street light nearby began to weaken as the sky soaked up the first hints of day from the hidden sun. She'd been wandering around all night, working things out, and she thought she was beginning to see them clearly at last.

And as she'd known, there would be a price to pay. And the price was simply this, that she had to take back the jacket and apologize.

So she'd phoned Helen's number from Liverpool first thing that morning and got Joe's address, without explaining why. Nor had she phoned Dad, nor had she found Robert. There was no shortage of things to feel guilty about, she thought, but one thing at a time, and this one first.

She pushed open the gate and went up the cracked path to the front door. The bell didn't work, so she knocked, and almost at once a high quavering cry arose from inside, like that of a mad child. She took a step back in fright.

Then there was the rumble of Joe's voice saying something in Welsh, and a key turned, and the door opened.

As far as his sullen features could manage it, they took on an expression of surprise. Before it could turn to anger, she said, 'I've brought your jacket back. It's all right. It's not damaged or anything. I've got it here in my rucksack. I just needed it for a few days. I'm sorry I took it like that. Can I . . .'

She faltered and stopped, because behind Joe she could see another figure, something out of a nightmare: a corpse, a ghoul, swathed in graveclothes, with a vacant mouth and hollow staring eyes. It plucked at Joe's sleeve, whimpering, and he turned and said in Welsh, 'It's all right, Mam, don't worry.'

A mother? Joe had a mother? Ginny could only stare. He turned back to her, and she said clumsily, 'Look, I'm sorry to bother you, but I really need to ask you something. Can I come in? It won't take long, honest . . .'

He considered heavily for a moment or two and said, 'Wait there.'

He shut the door again, and she heard their voices going back into the house. After a minute the door opened again, and she stepped inside, to the smells of fried food and cigarette smoke and unwashed clothes, and worse.

Joe's mother was sitting on a torn and greasy sofa, clutching a cushion as if it were a baby. She was wearing nothing but a pink nylon nightdress, the front of it stained with food, and a pair of yellow Garfield slippers. Her hair hung like grey rags from her bony head; she was toothless and senile and, Ginny saw, terrified of her.

'It's all right, Mam,' Joe said in Welsh. 'She won't hurt you. The little girl's come to see Joe. She won't hurt Mam. Don't worry.'

Ginny's head was swimming. She dragged the

jacket from the rucksack and held it out wordlessly, and he took it and slipped it on at once.

'Well?' he said.

'I wanted to ask you about my dad,' she said. 'Tony Howard.'

His mouth fell open. He was astonished, breathless. He couldn't speak.

She went on: 'It was you that told Benny that he'd been in jail, wasn't it?'

'Aye.'

'How did you know?'

'Because that's where I met him. *Duw*. It's *you* . . . Tony Howard . . . *Duw annwyl*, I never guessed . . .'

'What . . .?' Ginny's mouth was dry. She looked at the old woman on the sofa. 'Does your mam speak English?'

'She won't understand nothing. What d'you want to know?'

'What was he in prison for?'

'For kidnapping you,' Joe said. 'That was it, see.'

'*What?*'

'He stole you from somewhere and ran off with you. It was in all the papers. Everyone in the prison, they thought he was a nonce, till he fought back. Then they found out the truth.'

'What's a nonce?'

'You know, a man who molests kiddies. They

254

thought he was one of them. But then the story come out that it was his own kid, like, and there was nothing bad about it, and it was all right after that. See, prisoners, they hate men like that. Kill 'em if they could. You ought to ask him, not me. What did you take my bloody jacket for, anyway?'

'Because I . . . Oh, it's too complicated. I can't . . .'

'What d'you mean? Think I'm thick or something? Think I'm stupid?'

Behind Joe, sensing his slow-rumbling anger, his ancient mother was rocking back and forth, making crying sounds with her gaping mouth. Ginny looked from one to the other.

'No, it's not that – honest – I thought you got it from the broken bridge, Pont Doredig, and I—'

'The what? Pont Doredig? What's that?'

Ginny closed her eyes. 'It was a mistake. I heard this story about a car crash and someone stole a jacket from the car, and I – I thought it was that jacket. So I was going to take it back and . . . that's all. But I was wrong, I see now. I got it all wrong. I'm sorry. I shouldn't have taken it.'

'I bought this jacket,' he said. 'I never stole it.'

Ginny wondered if she could ask about Andy and why Joe was chasing him, why Andy had paid that money at the fair; but she was already feeling sick from the closeness and the smell, and besides, whatever business Andy had with Joe was dark and private. And Andy would always know how to look after himself.

Joe's mother was saying something in a high, tremulous voice. Ginny couldn't understand much, but she made out the word *black*. There was no getting away from it. Were all people crazy? This old woman was just another version of Grandma, a bit further gone, but fundamentally the same.

She turned to leave and heard Joe say in Welsh, 'Don't worry, Mam, she's not going to hurt you. She's a friend, she's Joe's friend, see, she's come to give Joe his jacket, she's a kind girl, don't you worry. We'll take you up to bed in a minute, make you happy again. Have some cocoa. Don't worry, now . . .'

Ginny quietly made her way to the front door and left. What he'd told her about Dad was less of a revelation than his tenderness to the deranged old woman who was his mother. That put everyone to shame. Why did everyone but Joe Chicago treat their relatives so badly?

But she itched to draw her. Like the picture Whistler made of his mother: the formal composition, the cool colours, but instead of the dignified old lady in her clean white bonnet and apron, this poor stained wreck in her nylon nightdress, the flesh withering on her arms, her swollen feet treading down the sides of the cheap yellow slippers.

To draw her grandparents. Grandad: The Man Who Looked Away. Her grandmother, possessed. The need to put them down on paper was almost an ache; she would, she would . . . And Joe, his great coarse giant's features, his greasy skin, the infinite gentleness in his eyes . . . How do you draw gentleness? What shape was that? What colour? Look at Rembrandt. Learn.

There was one more phone call to make. She found a booth by the harbour, put her phonecard in, and dialled. He snatched it up on the first ring.

'Dad?'

'Ginny – where the hell are you?'

'I'm in Porthafon. I'm coming home. Is Robert—'

'Robert's here, yes. Whereabouts are you?'

'By the harbour. There's a bus—'

'I'll come and get you. It'll be quicker.'

'We're going to have to talk, Dad.'

'I know. I know . . .'

'I'll be waiting in Davy Jones's Locker, OK?'

'I'll be there in half an hour.'

'Dad, can I talk to Robert? Is he there?'

'Yes, here he is. See you soon.'

The phone changed hands.

'Ginny?'

'Robert . . . Has he gone?'

'No, not . . . Yes. That was the front door. Where the hell did you go? Where've you been?'

'Oh, God, Robert. I'm sorry, leaving you and running out like that. I was just so confused . . . What did you do? You didn't stay there?'

'Not for long. She was crying and hitting herself with her fists – I've never seen anything like it – and he was just . . . He was dead scared; he was terrified. He gave me ten quid, you know. He . . . Just after you'd left, he called me into the front room while she was crying in the hall, and he shoved this money at me and said it was for both of us—'

'I don't want it.'

'Well, whatever. It was the only thing he could think of to do . . . But she said your mother was alive, didn't she? Was that why . . . and all that racist crap . . .?'

'Yeah. She's alive. I've seen her, Robert. I met her last night.'

'What? Where? What happened?'

She told him everything that had happened, and she found herself thinking: *It's true, he's my brother. I can tell him this, and he understands.*

She got to the end and said, 'And then . . . I just wandered about, thinking. It's crazy, you know. All

258

my life I've been wondering about my mother and then I find her and you know what? I can't feel anything at all. I thought I'd be so happy, I thought everything would be wonderful . . . And it isn't. Nothing's changed. Well, I've seen her paintings, and that's important—'

'Are they good?'

'They're . . . Oh, God, yes. She's the real thing. No question. But I mean, having seen them, right, I know how I've got to paint. Not because she's my mother, but because they . . . I can't explain. But as for her being a mother, forget it. Oh, and I found out why Dad was in jail. He kidnapped me. Probably from those nuns or whatever. At least, that's what Joe Chicago said.'

'You've spoken to Joe Chicago?'

'I've just been there. Robert, he was so kind to his mother . . . He looks after her. I never knew; I bet no one knows. She's senile, she can't feed herself or anything, and there he was, being all gentle . . . God, it's stupid; I'm crying just thinking about it . . .'

He was silent while she tried to gather herself together.

'So when did you get back?' she said. 'And Dad, what did you tell him?'

'I phoned him last night. I told him where we'd been. I stayed the night with someone I know up near Liverpool and came back first thing this morning. I thought he'd be angry, but he was just worried.'

'Yeah . . . Robert?'

'What?'

'I'm sorry.'

'What for?'

'Oh, that quarrel we had. Calling you whatever I called you.'

'Yeah, you went to town, didn't you.'

'I don't mean it any more. I didn't mean it then.'

'Nor did I.'

'I was just so wrapped up in *my* stuff, I couldn't . . .'

'Yeah. Well, I thought we . . . when we were there, at the grandparents' . . .'

'We were understanding each other then. Yeah. Right.'

'But what a pair . . . She's mad, isn't she? I mean insane?'

'Yeah. She must be. And all that Arthur and Kitty stuff . . . Do you remember Kitty?'

'Yeah. I hated her. I think *he* was the one, Arthur, he was the one who was bound up in it all, emotionally . . . She was as hard as nails.'

'Arthur and Grandad. It's so weird. And when, you know, when he was saying about Dad and my mother – it was as if no one had ever done that before, as if it was the end of the world . . .'

'The end of their world. Yeah, that's right. And the way she turned on him—'

'I remember that from when I was a kid,' Ginny said. 'You know I told you I'd seen her hit him, when I was staying there before. I saw them through the glass in the kitchen door? Well, I've just remembered she turned on him then exactly like that. If she'd had a knife, I swear she'd have used it. I can remember it so clearly, him just turning away holding his arm and saying, *Hush, for God's sake*. If he knew she was going to kill him, he'd ask her to do it quietly so they didn't disturb the neighbours.'

'Yeah, and spread some newspaper on the floor to catch the blood,' he said.

They were silent for a moment.

'It's really strange how different Dad is,' Ginny said. 'He's not like them at all.'

'Are you going to ask him about this kidnapping business?'

'Bloody right. Before I come home, I'm going to get *everything* out of him. I mean it. If not, that's the end for him.'

They talked a little more, but it didn't matter what they said; it was enough to be talking like friends. They said goodbye, and Ginny went to have some coffee in Davy Jones's Locker, sipping it slowly, looking out across the car park until she saw the white VW Golf come to a halt at the far side.

She shouldered her rucksack and went out to meet him.

Chapter Sixteen
Golden years, part two

'Hello, Dad.'

'Hello, Ginny.'

She clicked the seat belt on and settled the rucksack down between her feet as he put the car in gear and drove away. It was a good thing the night was hot; she would have missed that jacket otherwise, she thought.

He was silent beside her as they went out over the toll bridge and took the flat road south along the coast. There was a bright moon shining on the great hills to the left, the distant endless dunes far off to the right. Ginny realized that she was going to have to speak first, but at the very moment she thought that, he surprised her by saying, 'Robert told me you'd been to your grandparents'. And what happened? Was it much of a shock?'

'Dad . . . I've seen Maman. I spoke to her last night. You knew she was alive all this time, didn't you?'

Silence. His profile was clear in the dim light reflected from the road, and she stared at him mercilessly, trying to see any wavering, any weakness, any similarity to those doomed people in Chester. There was hardly any. He was quite different from them, and all she could see in his expression was sadness.

He slowed the car down, looking for somewhere to stop, and finally pulled up in the gateway to a field beside the road. He switched off the engine and the lights. All around them the wide night was silent; and then he began to speak.

'We should have done this years ago, shouldn't we? Talk, I mean. But things were OK for such a long time; I suppose we just talked about easy stuff like what are we going to have for supper and where shall we go on holiday . . . Anyway, we've come to it at last. The reason for all of this is quite simple, Ginny: it's fear. Fear is why it happened, fear is why I haven't talked about it. That's the reason for everything.

'I grew up afraid, Ginny. I was frightened every day of my life till I left home, and sometimes I'm still frightened now. Frightened of different things, but once you're marked . . .

'What was I afraid of most . . . Well, I was afraid my father would hit me, which he did. But not very afraid of that, and that stopped anyway as I got bigger. I was mainly afraid my mother wouldn't love me, I think. What would happen to me if she didn't love me any more I couldn't imagine, but it would be . . . it would be terrible.

'Some of the things that happened . . .

'I think the earliest memory I have, the very first thing I remember, is her beating me. Not smacking me or clouting me round the head but spanking me, and in public. I must have been about three. It was in a shop, some department store, and I'd taken something from one of those child-height displays and refused to put it back. I can't remember what it was, even, but I remember her tearing down my trousers, and my pants, and bending me over right there in the middle of the crowd and lashing at me with her open hand. And I remember screaming, "Daddy! Daddy!" and twisting my head to look for him, and reaching out with both arms, and I remember him standing a little way off looking in the other direction, though I knew he could hear me. I remember it all now, as if it had only just happened.

'Then when I was six or so she found me with my cousin Lucy. Lucy was a bit younger than me, and we were playing in the bedroom. And like all kids, I suppose, we were curious about each other's bodies, and we were comparing ourselves with each other in the most innocent way when the door opened suddenly and there was my mother. And her expression changed in a second. She seemed . . . it was as if she'd instantly gone mad, in a kind of explosion.'

He stopped. Ginny murmured, 'Yeah. We saw her do that . . .'

'That's the part that stays with me,' Dad went on, 'not Lucy's little body but the sheer terror I felt when my mother leapt at me. She sprang at me and snatched me up, half-clothed as I was, and she ran with me into the bathroom. I remember what I did, and this'll sound strange, but I swear it's true. I flung my arms around her neck and kissed her again and again and I cried, "I love you, Mummy, I love you . . ." Terror, you see. But it was no good. She tore my hands away and flung me down into the tub so hard I thought she'd killed me. Then she wrenched at the hot tap, and as the water came out, scalding, splashing down at me, she held me under the stream of it and said I was filthy, I was dirty scum inside and out, she was sickened and disgusted, I was unwholesome, I stank . . .

'But I loved her, Ginny, you see, I loved her because she was my mother, and because I loved her I thought she must be right, it must be true what she said. So all the time I was struggling to protect myself from the hot water I remember hoping that she wouldn't think I was struggling because I didn't love her, or that I was trying to hurt her, and I remember grabbing her sleeve, her red cardigan sleeve, and sobbing out that I was sorry, I was sorry, I was sorry. But she looked down at her arm with my tears and snivel all over it and she snatched it away, and pulled off the cardigan, and plunged that under the tap to scrub off the mess.

'Then she made me wait downstairs, out of the way, in the dining room, still without trousers and pants, and she rang my Auntie Mary, my father's sister. And a little later Auntie Mary came to take Lucy away. I've never seen her from that day to this. We were so friendly and happy together. I remember waiting at the dining room door, hoping to hear Lucy's voice, and not wanting to touch any of the furniture in case I dirtied it.

'One more memory. I had a teddy bear, the only soft toy I had. The rest of my toys – I had plenty of them – the rest were cars and trains and guns and construction kits. I was never short of things to play with, but I didn't love them like I loved my bear. He slept in my bed till . . . I don't know when it happened, but I'll never forget it, never. Not till I die.'

He swallowed hard. Ginny couldn't move. He

was clutching the steering wheel with both hands, staring ahead down the empty road. He went on:

'It was a winter night. I'd stolen a bar of chocolate from the newsagent's shop round the corner. I'd never done it before and I don't know why I did it then, but there I was, lying in bed with the light out, eating this chocolate, feeling smug because I had it and guilty because I knew I shouldn't. I stayed awake for a long time. And bit by bit the guilt grew and took over, and I hid the rest of the chocolate under my pillow and clung to Teddy.

'Then I started to cry. And my mother, who was coming up the stairs, she heard me and came in, and she saw the chocolate on my face and pulled the pillow away, and I knew what was going to happen, because her eyes flicked to Teddy and then she snatched him away from me.

' "He doesn't want Teddy any more," she said. "He wants chocolate instead. He's too old for Teddy. Teddy will have to be killed."

'Then she was gone, down the stairs in a flash, and I ran screaming after her, but she went out of the back door into the darkness and locked it behind her, and I heard terrible chopping sounds. They kept a little axe there, to chop the kindling wood. I clung to the back door, trying to drag it open, and then I fled, I ran into the sitting room, absolutely incoherent with terror, couldn't breathe, hardly, and I threw myself at my father, who was watching the television.

'But all he said was, "No, no, go back to bed, there's a good boy," and even in the state I was in I could tell he was frightened too. Then he looked up at the doorway and quickly pushed my hands away, because there she stood.

'D'you know, her face was full of sorrow. She opened her arms to me and because it was what I needed I ran to her and sobbed, and I found myself saying, "I'm sorry, I'm sorry . . ."'

'She took me upstairs and laid me back in my bed and explained – I remember her soft voice and the perfume she used to wear – she explained how when teddy bears weren't loved properly any more they had to be killed. Teddy had had to be chopped up, and it was very sad, but if I'd loved him more I wouldn't have wanted to eat chocolate instead. Then she kissed me and wished me happy dreams, and went out and shut the door and left me in the darkness.

'Till the moment I die I'll never forget that, that desolation, that misery. You might think I'd hate her, but feelings, I don't know, they're not that predictable, are they? In fact, after that, I was desperate with love and fear. I clung to her, I smothered her with affection, terrified that she'd think I didn't love her.

'Now I can see what she did to me, now I can see that she made me want to apologize to her for not loving her enough . . . Well, there are times when I could willingly go there and kill her. I still wake up now, a grown man, I still wake up in the night sweating with fear and rage and hatred. I can only excuse her by thinking that she's mad. But I can't forgive him. I'll never forgive him.

'Well . . . Anyway.

'So somewhere in the middle of all that they broke my confidence in myself, Ginny, and they never showed me how to repair it. Never thought to. They stamped me with fear so deep, so early on, I couldn't get rid of it.'

He stopped for a moment to pull out a handkerchief and wipe his eyes. Ginny wanted to touch him, to say something, but she felt helpless.

Then something absurd happened. The car windows were open, because of the heat, and at the same moment both Ginny and her father became aware of someone watching them, a presence. There was a face looking over the gate – a huge, solemn cow's face.

They laughed as the tension went, and hearing them the cow lumbered away nervously. Dad got out of the car and went to lean on the gate. Ginny joined him and presently the cow, curious again, came up slowly to gaze at them.

'I thought they put them inside at night,' Ginny said.

'It's having a strange night, like us. Ginny . . .'

He was looking away from her, and his voice was quiet in the wide night.

'I'm glad you went to Chester,' he said. 'It's made me tell you all this. You're like your mother.'

'How?'

'You make your mind up and then you act. It's what I should do. Should have done. I will . . . Thank you, Ginny love. I'm telling you all this because you deserve to know it, and to explain it to myself, I suppose . . . So you can see why I married Janet. There's no reason otherwise; I didn't love her . . . But her parents – Uncle Arthur and Auntie Kitty, as I had to call them – and mine, they had the whole thing worked out years in advance: I'd marry Janet, take over the firm, supply them with grandchildren. Oh, they didn't say it aloud, but it was there in everything they said and everything they did.

'And I didn't dare go against it, you see. It sounds incredible, I know, a grown man obeying his parents like a puppet, even against his own judgement. But that fear built into me over years, it was impossible

271

to resist, it was like defying gravity. Janet herself . . . I never knew what she thought. A smug, prim, narrow girl she was. A hard little nature, closed and greedy and . . . I could *see* it, and still I went through with the marriage. What a dream I was living in! A grown man, and the only thing I longed for was my mother's approval. I thought I didn't, but I did. I thought I'd grown beyond it, but I hadn't.

'So we got married, and then I met your mother. Anielle Baptiste. She was studying art. Came from a wealthy family, apparently. There'd been some kind of political trouble in the time of Papa Doc Duvalier; Anielle's father and mother had been exiled: they were living in Canada, I think . . . I don't know. She . . . I thought she was American at first, but she was intensely Haitian. An artist. My family thought art was something for women, or lefties, or homosexuals. Oh, and liars. They couldn't see what there was in it, so they thought people who said they could see something in it were lying. I suppose I'd thought that too, until I met Anielle. I knew she wasn't a liar. She was too honest for that. Too honest for me.

'I'd never met, never imagined there could be, anyone like her.

'And if I'd had the strength, if I hadn't had my confidence broken some long long time before, I'd have thrown Janet over and lived with Anielle. Maybe persuaded her to marry me. But I didn't. It was such a tangle: Janet was pregnant, Anielle was pregnant . . . and I didn't dare tell anyone about it until it was all too late. And then I told Janet. You can imagine the reaction.'

'They told us,' Ginny said. 'They said it knocked them sideways. It shattered everything.'

He nodded.

'Anielle was a Catholic, and there was no question of abortion, thank God. She disappeared and went into a Catholic nursing home to have you, and then . . . She just left. You see, my not leaving Janet, that was a betrayal she couldn't forgive. I don't forgive myself for it. If I'd lived with Anielle she might not have gone, might have stayed to be a mother . . . I don't know. There was the painting as well. She lived for that. Being a mother was something that happened to her; being a painter was something she was born to. She . . . she wasn't rejecting you, love. Don't blame her for leaving you.

'But she was so contemptuous of me that she didn't tell the nuns – the nuns who ran the nursing home – she didn't tell them my name. She just vanished. I didn't know where she'd gone, I didn't know if you'd been born safely, didn't know anything.

'And so when I finally found the children's home where they were looking after you and turned up claiming to be the father of this child . . . Well, six months had gone past. Why should they hand over a baby girl to a total stranger? Naturally they wouldn't, not until they'd made all kinds of checks. But I thought that if Janet . . . I thought that if she agreed to adopt you, if there was a home for you to go to, they'd be more likely to release you into my care. So that was when I told her about it.

'Ha. Fat chance. All that came of it was hysterics. I'd been unfaithful to her, I'd got a mistress, a black mistress, that was it, got a piccaninny child – that's the way she talked. She went straight round to her parents, and he, Uncle Arthur – I still called him that – he came to my parents as if it was something to do with them, as if I'd been a naughty boy and it was up to them to punish me for it . . . Or as if he'd bought me, one son-in-law, and I was faulty, and he was coming back to complain . . .

'Yes, when I look at it now, Ginny, it seems incredible, it seems impossible that grown people should behave like that, like Janet and Arthur and Kitty and my parents, and me, too, that we should all be acting like – what? Puppets? Not people, that's for sure. I was actually summoned, actually told to come and explain, come and apologize, they meant, come and grovel for forgiveness.

'But I couldn't stick that. I wouldn't behave like that. I told them all that you were my child, that I was going to look after you, and damn the rest of them. Janet could divorce me as soon as she liked; I'd pay her whatever maintenance she wanted to look after Robert. I . . . I didn't want him, any more than she wanted you. Then I walked out. I felt free. For the first time in my life, I felt free. Can you imagine that?

'So . . . I kept on struggling to get the social services to let me have you. All kinds of obstacles, all kinds of tests and questions and queries. Since it was a Catholic society looking after you by that stage, and since I wasn't living with my wife, that didn't make it any easier.

'In the end they agreed – the social services and the Catholic society between them and the courts and the priest and the bishop and the Pope for all I know – they agreed to let me have restricted access. I could have you for the occasional weekend, but no more. You were growing up, my little one, you were two and then you were three, and going from one foster parent to another and back to the home again . . . And then suddenly it stopped. I went to collect you one weekend and you were gone. You were with someone else, they said. A permanent placement.

'I've forgotten all the details, but it turned out that the difficulties I'd been having about getting you permanently were due to someone reporting me to the social services for . . . oh, cruelty, baby battering – that was the phrase then. The social services were in a cleft stick. They could see you were all right, but on the other hand they couldn't ignore rumours like that in case they turned out to be true. So they wouldn't let me have you. I couldn't believe it. I tried to get the name of whoever it was who'd been telling these lies, but of course they wouldn't pass on a thing like that.

'So there I was. Someone had stolen you. And once I'd calmed down and thought about it, I knew who it was at once.'

'Grandad? Grandma?' Ginny could hardly whisper. 'Was it them?'

'It was her.'

'And was that why I was staying with them?'

'That's right. What they thought they were doing, God only knows. They'd lied about me and then persuaded the fools in charge to let them look after you. After I'd walked out, after Arthur and Kitty had deserted them, they had nothing left, I suppose. Desperate. Well, I went mad. Thinking of the way

I'd grown up . . . you going through all that . . . I couldn't bear to think of it. So I went straight there and took you away.'

'Joe Chicago said . . . he said you were in prison. You kidnapped me and went to prison.'

'Oh, you've seen Joe? That's right, that's what happened. I kidnapped you. We travelled all over the country under different names. Six months, going from place to place. You probably don't remember any of it. Cheap rooms, flats, landladies, up and down the country . . . It couldn't last. And when I finally ran out of money and couldn't hide any more . . . Do you remember that cold morning in Norwich? Autumn morning, full of mist? No, probably not. The police station, the curious police-woman, the social worker who snatched you away and insisted on examining you there and then to see if you were being abused.

'Anyway, the arrangement my parents had had, that was a court order, and by taking you I'd violated it, you see. Contempt of court. More than that; I'd knocked the old fool down. Him. When I saw them I was shocked. Shrunk, they'd physically shrunk; they were huddled in this little narrow house where I'd spent my little frightened childhood; they were frightened themselves now . . . But he tried to bluster, tried to threaten me, and I lost my head and hit him. I should have done it years before. Still, it didn't sound good in court. They gave me six months, which my solicitor said was a bit steep. Lot of help he was. I was out after four, then I started the whole business again, only legally this time. I was determined. You were everything, you were my life. I wasn't going to give up.

'And eventually, at long last, eventually it came to the High Court and there was a sympathetic judge – what a miracle! He decided it once and for all. You were my child, I was your father, no question, I had custody, that was it. After four years, all finished in about four minutes.

'So we . . . started living, I suppose. Struggled. But at least we were together. Ginny . . . Tell me the truth now: was there even a moment when you thought I didn't love you?'

She couldn't speak. She could only shake her head.

'And when you were with them, when you were little . . . They didn't mistreat you, did they? They didn't frighten you?'

'No,' she said, swallowing hard. 'They didn't mistreat me.'

'I didn't think they would in just a few days. It would still be new for them; they wouldn't have time . . . And she could be kind, she could be generous sometimes. There was something to love there, under the madness . . .

'So time went by.

'I never told you the truth, because I was afraid to, you see. Ashamed. Everything I did before I decided to be your father, be responsible for you, I was ashamed of. I didn't want you to know about Janet or about any of it. So I invented a story and told you as much of the truth as fitted it. I told you that Maman had died because I thought it would be easier for you than thinking you had a mother who abandoned you. And now you tell me you've found her . . . It was bound to happen, I suppose. How was she? How did you find her?'

'I saw this advertisement in an art magazine,' Ginny said, brushing her eyes with the back of her hand. 'She was having an exhibition in a gallery in Liverpool. I rang them up, and the owner said I could come to the private view last night. And I saw her and I . . . I showed her the photograph. It was stupid of me, really. It wasn't the time. She knew it was her picture, but she wouldn't admit, it, she wouldn't admit who I was.'

'Did that upset you?'

'I thought it did. It's funny, I really thought it did, until I stopped wandering about feeling sorry for myself and realized what I did feel. And what I felt was: so what? It doesn't matter. I've never had her, so I can't miss her, really. Her pictures are wonderful; that's the important thing. I don't have to be her daughter to see those, though.'

'Did she look well?'

'Oh, yes. She looked . . . very strong and independent.'

'Yes. She was that. I'm glad she's doing well. And I'm glad she's seen you too, even if she didn't want to. She'll be proud of you.'

Ginny doubted that. Dad went on:

'And anyway, that's how it would have stayed. But then Janet got ill and Robert was going to need somewhere to go . . . He could have gone to his grandmother, Kitty, in Spain. But she didn't want him; she made that perfectly clear. She was a detestable woman. My mother was mad, perhaps, but Kitty was just cold, hard, greedy . . . both of them much stronger than their husbands. Arthur and my father, they were the real marriage. That was the real bond. The wives weren't nearly so close.'

'That's what Robert said,' Ginny told him.

'He's right. He sees a lot, Robert . . . What was I talking about?'

'About Robert,' Ginny said. 'Needing somewhere to go.'

'Oh, yes. Well, he wasn't wanted with Kitty, and

as for my parents, that was out of the question. The only option was to live in some residential home up in Liverpool while he did his A Levels. When Wendy Stevens came that day and told me about it, I knew I'd have to offer to have him here. I was responsible for him. So that's when it all began to unravel. I should have told you everything straight away. I should have told you everything from the beginning. Stupid of me. But I was afraid, you see. That's at the heart of it.'

They stood for a while in silence. Not a single car had gone past; they had the night to themselves. The cow had wandered away, and far away over the flat fields Ginny could hear an owl cry.

'Actually,' Ginny said, 'there was something else that started it for me. Rhiannon's sister, Helen, she'd heard from someone that you'd been in prison. When I heard that, I thought no, it's impossible. But it made me start wondering . . . I went to see Joe Chicago tonight, before I rang home. I . . . I pinched his jacket, you see. I thought he'd stolen it, and I wanted to . . . give it back in some way. But I realized he hadn't stolen it after all, so I went to see him. He was looking after his mother. He told me why you were in prison. I suppose I could have asked him a long time ago if I'd dared. I just thought he was so dangerous.'

Dad didn't speak for a while. Then he said, 'Yeah . . . Helen. I had no idea she was Rhiannon's sister. Well, it's a small place. And poor old Joe. I see him sometimes in town and give him a few quid. He's harmless. But looking like that, he hasn't got much in his favour. Ginny . . . I'm sorry.'

She was a little surprised. 'What for?'

'For not telling you.' He paused. 'For all this.'

She thought of the years when there'd just been the two of them, when she'd been the queen of the world and he'd been the king; she thought of the breakfast ladies; she thought of that little boy her father had been; she thought of the desolation of his parents, knowing themselves abandoned and hated, and knowing why; she thought of Robert and his cold, hard, dying mother; she thought of Dad in jail for her sake, and her not knowing anything about it; she thought of Joe Chicago's mother. A sense of the vast loneliness and sadness of being human brushed past her. The world was huge, after all. She'd been very lucky.

Then without knowing how it happened, she was crying on his shoulder, sobbing for all of them, and his arms were round her as they'd always been.

After a while Ginny sighed a shaky sigh and they stood apart.

'You know,' she said, confessing, 'I thought I was

so hard done by . . . and I wasn't at all. Robert's much worse off than me. So were you. I just didn't realize. But once I felt things were shaky underneath . . . well, I couldn't trust anything. There were all sorts of other people who knew things about me that I didn't and I had to find out, Dad. I had to. And now I see . . .'

They got back in the car. Ginny found herself yawning. The lights of a truck lit up the interior from behind them, and the heavy vehicle roared steadily past on its way to the south, laden with Mr Alston's garden furniture to pay for more bricks for his beach house, perhaps, or with cases of wine for the Yacht Club.

'You know,' she said, 'I never even asked if they did the ton.'

'The what?'

'In the Yacht Club. A hundred dinners. They probably did, though. I think they need another waiter. D'you think Robert would like a job?'

'You'd better ask him,' he said, starting the engine. 'Let's go home.'

Chapter Seventeen
The morning train

Ginny woke up long before six. She knew it was early before she looked at the clock; the sun was already shining in through the gap in the curtains, but the air was cool and fresh, fresher than it had seemed for days.

And because it was so long since she'd been on the beach, Ginny found herself longing for the edge of the water once more, the shore of her kingdom. She got up quickly, washed her face and cleaned her teeth, and put on shorts and T-shirt and trainers. The house was still, the others both asleep. She left through the kitchen and ran down the lane.

In the pearly light, her kingdom looked like one of those dreamy beaches painted by Salvador Dali: tiny bizarre details in an infinite limpidity. The ribs of the old fishing boat sticking up out of the mud in the estuary, the station cat curled up asleep on a beer barrel outside the Yacht Club kitchen, a washing line strung between the rafters of Mr Alston's house, with Dafydd's or Andy's dingy shirts and socks hanging in the open loft – she saw them all bathed in the same benevolent clarity. There was no one about, no one awake, and hers were the first footprints on the beach.

She took off her shoes and left them at the edge of the soft sand before going down to the water. The tide was nearly out, and the air was so still that there was nothing to stir the sea into waves. It was smooth and glassy as far as Ginny could see; in her imagination she saw this surreal calm extending out past the southern coast of Ireland and on into the ocean, south and west for thousands of miles, through the Sargasso Sea and over the lost continent of Atlantis, where sea serpents coiled among the ruined temples, until it touched the shores of Haiti.

Where the *loa* lived. Where Baron Samedi had come from. They were real; you had to respect them, even when they were wrong about things. All of that was dark and confusing, but it was part of what she was. Maybe art itself was a kind of voodoo, possessing you, giving you supernatural power, letting you see in the dark.

With the sun on her back, she waded into the chilly water, wriggling her toes down into the sand, sensing the presence of little curious nibbling things deep out of sight. She wandered slowly along, knee-deep, thinking about the broken bridge, and about why she'd been so affected by the story.

Because it *was* about her. She was the baby, the warm fur-lined jacket was her mother, and Joe Chicago . . . Joe Chicago wasn't death; he was art.

She stood still. Now the story made perfect sense. It was art that had taken her mother away, because art had no conscience; it demanded, it was cruel, it took what it wanted brutally and paid no heed to the consequences. Or (as Rhiannon would say) it wasn't kind, it was sexy.

Ginny wandered a little further, the mild water stirring around her legs, and reached down to cool her hands, lifting it and letting it trail down in glittering drops. Kind or sexy – was this a division that split the world in two? Was Rhiannon right? Did everything have to be either kind and ineffective or sexy and heartless?

And as for her, she'd protested to Rhiannon that it must somehow be possible to be both. Well, how did she rate? She remembered trying to comfort Helen in the little spare room at Jubilee Terrace and moving her leg to improve the balance of the composition: nothing very kind there. She remembered Robert's words in that terrible quarrel – bitter hurting words, but they were true. Part of her *was* cold and arrogant; part of her *was* indifferent to those who were untalented.

Arrogant, indifferent . . . But sexy, as in sex? She

thought of her one attempt to become a lover, and grimaced.

How unlikeable she was.

But at least, she found herself arguing feebly, there was no envy in her. When she saw talent or genius she didn't resent its not being hers; she rejoiced in it wherever it was. It was the most important thing in the world . . .

She heard her mother again: *Painting isn't the most important thing, but it'll have to do till we find out what is.* She'd meant *for us. For people like us. For artists.* She'd acknowledged that connection, if nothing else.

Ginny turned around and walked slowly back the other way, the sun now full on her face and breast and arms. She wasn't alone on the beach any more; there was someone at the far end, coming towards her. A boy. Robert. She waved, and he waved back.

Well, even if she was an artist, she could still be a sister, do whatever sisters did. She wondered whether to tell Robert about what Dad had said in the car, in the dark and silence of the night, but she swiftly decided not to. That was a secret. It was an acknowledgement of the closeness they'd had, she and Dad, and she'd respect it. Besides, there was no need for Robert to hear anything that reflected badly on his mother, who might have been narrow and prim and greedy like Kitty but who had just painfully died, after all.

Or was concealing it from Robert no better than Dad's concealing things from her for so long? It was hard to say. She hoped she could get it right.

She bent to pick up her shoes as his shadow fell across them.

'Hi,' she said.

'Hello,' said Glyn Williams.

She looked up, blinking in astonishment. Yes, it was Glyn, not Robert at all, and for a moment she didn't know what to say.

'What's the matter?' he said.

'I thought you were someone else. Sorry, I didn't mean . . .'

He shrugged, smiling, and half turned away, and she fell in with his unspoken invitation and walked along beside him to the mouth of the estuary.

'You're up early,' she said.

'I help out with the horses,' he said. There was a riding stable in the village, where tourists paid to sit in hard hats and be slowly led up into the hills and down again by girls in jodhpurs.

'I can't see you doing that, somehow,' she said.

'I don't do the pony-trekking stuff. I go there first thing before the tourists come. I'm in the shop most of the day anyway. I do it so I can get free rides.'

'D'you ride, then? I didn't know . . .'

'Yeah. What about you?'

'I've never tried.'

'You ought to come. I'll take you out. You won't have to go in a line with a lot of little kids.'

She looked at him. Was this a date? Was someone asking her to go out with him? She was suddenly conscious of her bare legs, her thin T-shirt with nothing under it; and of his dark-red curly hair, his half-innocent, half-sardonic smile, like Andy's but more complicated, stronger, more subtle. And she was conscious of her unlikeableness. She felt so shy that she could hardly breathe.

'Well, why not?' he said. 'I'll teach you to ride.'

'No reason. Thanks. Yeah. I'd like that.'

They walked on slowly.

'How's your brother getting on?' he said.

'Oh, Robert. Yeah, fine. You know his mam died recently? That's why he's here. It was hard at first. It probably will be for a while, but he's OK.'

They reached the breakwater, a stone wall with a concrete path on the top just wide enough for two people to walk abreast. She stopped to put on her shoes before jumping up to join him, and they wandered along toward, the end. To their left was the glistening sand of the empty lagoon, to their right the seaweed-covered rocks at the foot of the breakwater. Ahead, across the narrow mouth where the river entered the sea, was the widest stretch of dunes on the whole coast: miles of high tumbled sand hills laced through with marram grass, and a beach where you could find a billion perfect shells. Ginny seldom went there, near as it was, because swimming across the mouth was safe only at low tide and the journey all the way round by land was miles. But now they had a boat, she remembered suddenly. It would be easy.

'Can you sail?' she said.

'No. Why?'

'Well, I can't either, but my dad bought a boat a couple of weeks ago. When I've learned to sail, I'll teach you,' she said, daring. 'In exchange.'

'All right! That's a bargain. Hey, I haven't seen you around for a few days. You been away?'

'Yeah. Robert and I went to Chester to see our grandparents. But I've been busy, you know . . .'

'What, drawing?'

'How d'you know about my drawing?'

'Well, don't sound so defensive. *Cet animal est très méchant—*'

'*Quand on l'attaque, il se défend!*' she finished. 'Yeah. Sorry. You weren't even attacking me.'

'Anyway, you're not an *il*, you're an *elle*.'

'Yeah, but that wouldn't work, 'cause it'd be *méchante*, and it wouldn't rhyme.'

'*Touché*,' he said. 'I know about your drawing because, first, Rhiannon told me, and second, I saw your stuff in the Art Room, and third, I saw you out on the top road drawing the other evening. I was going to come and say hello, but you'd scarpered by the time I got there.'

What a difference that might have made, she thought. What a difference this was making now. They reached the end of the breakwater, and Glyn sat down.

'I brought you a present,' he said, and she noticed that he was carrying a paper bag.

'What? Me? Oh . . .'

Is that all you can say? she thought. *Don't be so bloody incoherent, girl. Inarticulate. Whatever. Say thank you.*

'Thanks,' she said, sitting down awkwardly beside him.

He was taking out two kiwi fruit and a clasp knife. 'I saw you from the stables,' he said, 'and I thought you looked hungry, so I raided the shop.' He cut the fruit in half and gave her two pieces, and they ate the delicate flesh out of the skins, wiping away the juice with the backs of their hands.

'I love kiwi fruit,' she said. 'How could you see I looked hungry?'

'I couldn't. It was just an excuse. You didn't look very happy, though.'

He was close enough for her to see the flecks of green in his eyes, and for a long confusing moment she couldn't tell whether he was kind, or sexy, or both.

'Well, I am,' she said. 'Honest. I wasn't, but that's' – she gestured vaguely – 'over now,' she finished.

'You're coming back to join the rest of us?'

'Did it seem like that?'

'Yeah. Rhiannon said it was your artistic temperament.'

'There's no such thing!'

'Well, it can't have been that, then,' he said, 'but I won't ask if you don't want me to.'

She looked at him again. 'Do you really want to know?'

'Yeah. I'm interested. 'Cause I like you. And I mean, now we've had breakfast together, we ought to get to know each other better. Wouldn't be proper otherwise, would it?'

'No,' she agreed smiling. 'So you want to know what I've been doing?'

'Well, not *now*, necessarily. Not all at once. You could start this afternoon when we go riding.'

'This after*noon* already?'

'Why not?'

There was no reason. She shrugged, quite unable to keep that smile off her face.

'OK,' she said.

This was novel. This was better than unexpected kiwi fruit, even. Ginny saw something flash beyond Glyn's shoulder and watched as the sun caught the windows of the morning train crossing the little bridge outside Stuart's house and slowing down to stop at the station.

He saw where she was looking. '*Duw*, is that the time?' he said. 'I'll have to get a move on. I'll see you later, then. At the stables, about two o'clock, all right?'

She nodded, feeling dopey from her smile to her trainers, and watched him go.

Glyn. Well. Wow.

She sat at the end of the breakwater hugging her knees as her kingdom came to wakefulness around her, intact, rich, alive in all its details, from the scuttling little crabs among the rocks below her to the station cat yawning and stretching outside the Yacht Club, from the mother-of-pearl water to the great green presence of the hills.

There was so much to do.

Apologize to Angie Lime and Mr Calvert, first,

for missing a couple of days without letting them know.

Talk to Rhiannon. (That could last for days.)

Get to know Robert. Learn to sail.

Write to her mother. No. Yes. Maybe. Or write, but not mail it. Sort out what she thought. Talk to Glyn about it . . .

Go and see Helen. Explain.

Think about her grandparents. Maybe one day it would be possible to meet them somewhere neutral, somewhere safe and public. Maybe she and Dad and Robert could do it together. The old people were so desperate and unhappy; maybe everyone could just begin to be normal with each other, and be a family for the first time.

Talk to Stuart about her mother's paintings.

Those paintings . . . She realized that she was still dazed by them. *The Death of Colonel Paul* was an arrangement in red and yellow, a stunning one, but it wasn't only that; it was about human beings as well, about suffering and justice and greed. It cut through all the jargon and the labels and the boxes of abstraction and post-modernism and neo-expressionism; it was technically dazzling and it showed something true; it was the way a person could paint and be faithful to everything she knew, to Europe and to Africa, to academic discipline and to voodoo. If her mother's absence all these years had made it possible for her to show Ginny that, then it had been worth it, Ginny thought.

Her hand itched for a pencil. And that afternoon she was going riding with Glyn . . . She marvelled. Maybe she wasn't so unlikeable. Maybe you could be an artist *and* have a boyfriend. Anything was possible, really. Even being kind as well as sexy.

She stood up and stretched. The sun was hot already; the morning train, having unloaded its newspapers, was moving out towards Porthafon, and in the bright clear air Ginny could hear a crate of bottles being put down somewhere outside the Yacht Club, the newsagent's van turning into the station, distant voices calling.

She turned to run up to the house. As she passed the station, she waved to the porter and the newsagent, and to Harry Lime, who stood there scratching in the Yacht Club kitchen doorway, and their voices mingled. *Bore da*, good morning, *bore da*, Ginny, good morning, good morning.

Philip Pullman
The Butterfly Tattoo

Chris Marshall met the girl he was going to kill on a warm Oxford night in early June . . .

Chris loved her the moment he first set eyes on her – beautiful, secretive Jenny who rushed headlong into his life. Fate brought her to him, and fate would mercilessly come between them to drive their innocent love affair down a dark road of danger and betrayal. And make Chris discover that truth and trust are not the simple ideals he once believed . . .

'Grippingly readable . . . a tragic thriller' *TES*

'A work of undisputed and breathtaking excellence'
Books for Keeps

A selected list of titles available from Macmillan Children's Books

The prices shown below are correct at the time of going to press. However, Macmillan Publishers reserves the right to show new retail prices on covers which may differ from those previously advertised.

PHILIP PULLMAN

| The Butterfly Tattoo | 0 330 39796 6 | £4.99 |

CELIA REES

Truth or Dare	0 330 36875 3	£4.99
The Bailey Game	0 330 39830 X	£4.99
The Wish House	0 333 94739 8	£10.99

SHARON CREECH

Bloomability	0 330 39784 2	£4.99
Chasing Redbird	0 330 39782 6	£4.99
Walk Two Moons	0 330 39783 4	£4.99
Absolutely Normal Chaos	0 330 39781 8	£4.99
The Wanderer	0 330 39292 1	£4.99

All Pan Macmillan titles can be ordered from our website, www.panmacmillan.com, or from your local bookshop and are also available by post from:

**Bookpost
PO Box 29, Douglas, Isle of Man IM99 1BQ**

Credit cards accepted. For details:
Telephone: 01624 677237
Fax: 01624 670923
Email: bookshop@enterprise.net
www.bookpost.co.uk

Free postage and packing in the United Kingdom